Christmas by the Book

a novel

Beverly King

Covenant Communications, Inc.

Published by Covenant Communications, Inc.
American Fork, Utah

Printed in the United States of America
First Printing: August 1995

01 00 99 98 97 96 95   10 9 8 7 6 5 4 3 2

ISBN 1-55503-845-x

Library of Congress Cataloging-in-Publication Data

King, Beverly.
    Christmas by the Book / Beverly King.
    p. cm.
    ISBN 1-55503-845-X
    1. Title.
PS3561.I4733C47 1995
813'.54--dc20   95-4809
                                        CIP

DEDICATION

This book is for my father, Clair King, who has always supported my dreams, and for my mother, Emma King, the first published writer I ever met.

Chapter 1

Letter from Spindrift Farm—

To me Christmas at Spindrift Farm is like no other on earth. Snow has always been the major ingredient for that special Christmas feeling, and by December 25th we usually have several feet of snow that has drifted across the meadows and robed the trees in glistening array. The pale winter light gives us the feeling of a mystical Northern kingdom.

Christmas celebrations are a tapestry woven with memories which often stretch back to our childhoods. Each cookie I bake, each carol I sing, each gift I wrap reminds me of the times I've done this before.

Simon Kent lifted his eyes from *Today's Home* and stared through the plane window at the blue sky filled with cumulus clouds. At the moment, snow and Christmas were incomprehensible. Six months spent as a hostage in a steaming South American jungle had numbed his feelings to anything but being free.

He looked at *Today's Home* again. He'd never read a home decorating magazine before, but by the time the stewardess had gotten to his row with the magazines, there wasn't much of a selection—*Newsweek* and *Today's Home*. So while he'd have preferred sports, he'd picked decorating. He had no desire to read about himself, and he had until January 1 to catch up on world problems. For right now he wanted to avoid the nitty-gritty of real life.

Flipping the pages back to the articles, he continued reading. This Laura Reynolds wasn't too bad. Her enthusiasm about living on a farm reminded him of his grandmother. He couldn't ever remember meeting anyone of his own generation who felt the same way, and he certainly didn't. He'd learned enough about farming to know that city life was for him. He'd loved staying with his grandparents on their farm when he was a kid, but as he grew older he'd preferred living in the East. Later his job with First Federal had taken him all over the world. But no more assignments south of the border, because he didn't want to give the rebels another chance to capture him. Enough was enough. Give him the good old USA, preferably midtown Manhattan.

An overwhelming wave of nostalgia hit him. Closing his eyes, he relaxed against the firm cushions of the airplane seat. After years of glitzy celebrations, suddenly he yearned for a homespun family Christmas. But his only brother was in the Orient, and they wouldn't be reunited until after New Year's. So this year he'd be spending Christmas with friends at a ski resort; there'd be nothing homey about it. Oh, they'd have snow all right, but the main focus would be skiing. Now after six months away from anything even remotely resembling home, the last things he wanted were days spent on the slopes and nights at *apres-ski* parties.

The Laura Reynolds' column brought back the forgotten childhood memories of Christmas—searching the Montana mountains to find just the right tree, inhaling the wonderful smells of his mother's baking, and spending Christmas Eve wide-eyed with anticipation.

Then there were the ward Christmas parties. Excited by the prospect of Santa arriving, the kids tore around the cultural hall, impervious to their parents' demands that they sit down and be quiet. He hadn't realized until his father became bishop that part of the calling was to be Santa.

He'd never been interested in the "Happy Homemaker" type. Not that he'd ever met many—they hadn't attended Princeton or Wharton Business School in any great abundance. His taste had always run to ambitious, career women. Right now, however, Laura Reynolds sounded pretty good to him. Undoubtedly she was too old and, obviously from the column, too married. He sighed with regret.

Chapter 2

Letter from Spindrift Farm—

Many people decorate with a different color each year, choosing whatever's in vogue. Not me. I find it impossible to use anything but red and green. These colors are an integral part of the mosaic of my past celebrations.

Sitting on the floor of her Salt Lake City condominium, surrounded by Christmas presents yet to be wrapped, Amanda Richards paid scant attention to the hum of her TV and the 10:00 news. At this time of year the last things she wanted to hear about were hotel fires and arms negotiation talks. As far as she was concerned this was the season to be jolly. She loved the sights and sounds of Christmas, although not necessarily the Currier and Ives version.

With a half-harried, half-contented sigh, she picked up the miniature cast-iron sleigh she'd bought last August for her grandmother who loved antiques, particularly old ornaments. Sorting through the tissue paper, Amanda chose a bright fushia. The carnival colors of her gift wrap reflected her plans to celebrate the holiday in St. Thomas with her parents. Christmas in the Caribbean. After the cold, snowy weather of the last two weeks, she felt warmer just thinking about it.

Glancing at the TV through the fringe of her long blond hair, she watched a half dozen television reporters stick their microphones into someone's face.

"One final question. On a personal note, do you have any special plans for Christmas?"

"I'll be skiing in Utah, but—" the man gave a short laugh— "if I had my way I would be spending it with Laura Reynolds at Spindrift Farm."

What? Amanda's head shot up. *Who wants to spend Christmas with Grandmother Nonnie?* Leaning back on her arms, she focused on the screen. A gaunt man, whose beard and hair were heavily streaked with gray, stared back at her.

"Laura Reynolds?" The reporter sounded as surprised as Amanda felt, and the tone of his question indicated that he thought he might have a human interest story here.

The man waved a magazine into the view of the camera. "I read her column on the flight home. And after six months in a thatched hut, I'm ready for some nostalgia. Can you think of anything more American than Christmas at Spindrift Farm?"

Amanda remembered who Simon Kent was. She'd read about him in the newspaper. An international banker, Kent had just been rescued from a South American jungle by Protestant missionaries. She shook her head in surprise. In his ill-fitting clothes and his long gray beard, he looked more like a hermit than a successful business man.

How did one survive imprisonment in a jungle for that long? She didn't think she could have. She might have been able to stand the heat, since she'd always hated the cold, but she liked modern conveniences, and somehow she doubted a jungle hut had hot—and—cold running water, let alone a flush toilet.

"Also tonight...."

The camera flicked back to the news center and the anchor droned on, but Amanda couldn't get Simon Kent out of her mind. So he wanted a good, old-fashioned, Laura Reynolds Christmas. A holiday spent that way was, in her opinion, vastly overrated. She preferred the white sands of the Caribbean to the white snow of Utah. And her ideal holiday meal consisted of smoked turkey and fresh vegetables served in the hotel dining room. Her father was in the diplomatic corps, and she and her parents customarily met at Christmastime somewhere warm. Other more conventional souls like Nonnie could carry on the White Christmas tradition.

Five years ago, as the new editor of *Today's Home*, Amanda had persuaded her grandmother to write a monthly column on country living. Laura Reynolds's column had become a hit. Last year Nonnie's book, *Harvest Time at Spindrift Farm*, had almost made the *New York Times* best-seller list.

Amanda could see the headlines now: "Released Hostage Spends Dream Christmas with Laura Reynolds." No, make that: "*Today's Home's* Laura Reynolds." She smiled with satisfaction. This would make wonderful publicity. A magazine could never have too many readers, especially a regional magazine that had just gained a toehold in the national market. That ought to boost circulation.

Even better, *People* magazine would probably be interested in running a two-page spread on it. Amanda knew that her grandmother, warm and generous to a fault, wouldn't mind having Simon Kent for a guest. The renowned Laura Reynolds would make sure she gave him a Christmas he would always remember.

What possibilities! Excitement surged through her. New ideas to promote the magazine always gave her a rush. She almost took up her notebook to start jotting down ideas, but she had to finish wrapping her presents if she were going to be ready to leave on time. An hour later she scrambled stiffly to her feet to make a few notes of things to do and people to contact tomorrow.

The next morning Amanda stood in the foyer of *Today's Home* and admired the decorating abilities of her staff. The magazine staff had remodeled the historic home on east First South in Salt Lake for a series of articles that they later compiled into a book. Afterwards, they had moved the editorial offices here, which was a wonderful atmosphere for the magazine.

The reception area, her office, and the so-called test kitchen (a.k.a. the staff lounge) took up the first-floor space. The interior design department claimed the second floor and the other magazine offices were on the third. The entire area was now decorated for the pages of the December issue. Fresh pine garlands wound around the banisters of the magnificent cherry wood staircase, which curved grandly into the entrance hall. Renaissance angels garbed in crimson and gold highlighted the greenery. American folk-art angels hung along one paneled wall.

Inside the reception room, pine swags arched gracefully above stained glass windows, and nativity scenes nestled on the bookshelves and tables. The room was calm and serene—at six in the morning, who would expect anything else? Amanda usually arrived before the others, although seldom this early. Thoughts of Simon Kent had wakened her at four a.m., then raced through her mind, making further sleep impossible. Finally she got up and came to work.

The job as editor-in-chief of *Today's Home* had actually come to Amanda through a friend of her father's although her experience as an editorial assistant for a publisher in New York City had helped. During her five-year tenure at the helm, *Today's Home* had gone from a regional publication to one with a national presence. Now if she could just solidify the magazine's position, maybe she could relax.

The polished wooden floor creaked as Amanda crossed the reception area to put her frozen dinner in the lounge refrigerator. Even this room hadn't escaped Christmas. Pink poinsettias decorated the three tables, and large pink velvet bows were attached to the backs of the twelve pink-cushioned chairs. A large refrigerator, an apartment-size range, and the ever-popular microwave oven stood along the west wall. A festoon of pink poinsettias and laurel leaves hung over each of the windows. Christmas cookie jars arranged on the counters added warmth to the room. Fortunately for her waistline, they were empty. Nonnie tested her recipes at Spindrift Farm on her restaurant style stove and brought the results here for an eager staff to sample.

Entering her office, which had originally been the living room, Amanda dropped her briefcase in the nearest chair, then pulled off her gloves and coat and hung them on a brass coat tree just inside the door. In deference to Amanda's love of the untraditional, Ellen, the interior decorating editor, had put peach silk moiré ribbon with flamboyant variegated-peach silk roses on a fir tree. She had repeated the bows and roses on the mantelpiece, over the tall stately windows, and on the bookshelves. With the apricot and gold furnishings, the room looked terrific.

Since it would be a couple of hours before she could start calling people to put her plans in motion, she picked up the articles from her pending file. On the top was the April letter from Spindrift Farm. Nonnie had written on the popularity of raising old-fashioned roses. She herself actually did this kind of thing, but Amanda knew she hadn't inherited her grandmother's talents in gardening. Someone had once given her a small potted rosebush, which had died within days. No, reading about growing them was infinitely better!

She edited three articles before the staff started arriving, and the day officially began. Even though Nonnie was not a morning person, Amanda figured eight shouldn't be too early to call. So she quit marking time and picked up the phone. After ten rings, when Amanda was just about to hang up, she heard her grandmother's sleep-filled voice.

"I'm sorry, Nonnie. It sounds like I woke you."

"That's all right, dear, I needed to get up anyway. What is it?"

Amanda's eyes gleamed with excitement. She could just imagine Nonnie's enthusiasm. "Did you see Simon Kent on the news?"

"Yes, I did. I was going to call you last night, but I thought it might be too late. Your granddad's amenable to fulfilling Simon's wish. Personally, I can't think of a more gratifying way to spend Christmas." Now she was beginning to sound more like her sunny self.

9

"Oh, Nonnie, would you?"

"Of course. Just imagine that old man, a prisoner in some primitive hut for nearly a year, subsisting on corn meal and beans or whatever they fed him. No radio, no television—not that they're important, but—imagine, nothing to read, coping with heat and rain and bugs and snakes. Really, his situation must have been intolerable."

"I agree. I don't think I could have stood it."

"He comes home, filled with longing for the things he's missed. I'm sure he wants his life to return to normal." Now Nonnie's voice became dramatic. "But he also wants something more, something to offset the loneliness and misery. He wants what only Laura Reynolds can give him."

"Exactly." Amanda smiled with satisfaction. She'd known she could count on her grandmother.

"Would you find out where he's staying?"

"That won't be a problem. I'll put Becki right on it." Switching the phone to her other ear, Amanda picked up a pen. "What else can I do to help?"

"Now, dear, you know I've got it all under control. I made a list last night of what I needed to do."

Amanda hesitated. "Would you mind having a photographer take pictures for *Today's Home* and, if I can arrange it, *People* magazine?"

Nonnie was not shy. "I'd love it. And it would be wonderful publicity for both the magazine and my book."

"Nonnie, you're fantastic," Amanda said enthusiastically. "Listen, I'd be happy to stay here and help you." That's the least she could do.

"Now, dear, you know I don't need your help, and I am certainly not going to deprive you of the Caribbean."

Amanda breathed a sigh of relief, but she felt guilty leaving this all on Nonnie. "I'll get Mr. Kent's hotel and call you back. Love you."

Before she could buzz her, there was a light knock, and her

assistant Becki entered. "Did you see Simon Kent on TV last night?"

She didn't wait for Amanda's answer before she burst out, "What fantastic publicity for the magazine!" At two years out of college, the petite, brunette twenty-three-year-old had the exuberance of a cheerleader, which she tempered with hard work.

Amanda smiled. "Besides that, Nonnie is inviting him for the holidays."

Becki looked completely stunned. "Wow!" she breathed.

Amanda grinned at her. Every time Becki used that word Amanda was still startled that it came out of the mouth of an otherwise sophisticated and sharp-looking young woman like Becki. "I need you to check the hotels in Park City and try to locate Simon Kent."

Thirty minutes later, Becki had discovered the hotel and learned that Simon Kent would be arriving in the early afternoon. Amanda relayed the information to Nonnie who was getting ready to go shopping in Salt Lake. She was one person who always did her Christmas shopping in advance.

"I hate to have you coming in from Charleston. After the snow we've had, I-80 through Parley's Canyon is a mess. Couldn't you shop closer to home?"

"Now, dear, it's only a couple of hours and you know the only place I ever shop is ZCMI's. Don't worry, your granddad's taking me, and we'll be perfectly safe. I don't want to put off getting Christmas gifts for Simon and the photographer."

Well, that was that! Once Nonnie made up her mind, there was no changing it. Leaving everything in her grandmother's capable hands, Amanda left for an editorial meeting in the conference room.

The entire editorial board was enthusiastic about the Simon Kent promotion. Although the art department recommended Paul Merritt to do the photography, Amanda had her reservations about his being a good house guest. Gruff and sardonic, he'd recently gone through a divorce. Which meant, Amanda knew, that he was likely to be at loose ends and willing to come.

Sitting at her desk after lunch, Amanda reached for the phone just as it rang.

"Amanda, we've got trouble here."

At her grandfather's words, fear gripped her. She knew that he was never one to exaggerate. "What's happened?" she asked breathlessly

"We're at the emergency room at LDS Hospital," he said hurriedly. "Your grandmother slipped on some ice."

Amanda hardly dared to ask. "Is she all right?"

"She's being x-rayed right now. We won't know until we get the results. Can you come up?"

"Be there in five minutes." Slamming down the phone, Amanda hurriedly slipped on her coat and grabbed her purse. She briefly explained to Becki what had happened, then hurried to her car.

At the hospital she backed her car against a No Parking sign, turned her wheels to the curb, and ran for the entrance.

Inside she found her grandfather, pale and shaken, waiting in a curtained-off cubicle for Nonnie. After years as a defense attorney in Salt Lake, he'd just recently retired. He'd always wanted to live in the house where he'd been born, so he and Nonnie had moved back to Heber Valley. Nonnie loved everything about country living, except not having ZCMI a few blocks away.

Touching her granddad's shoulder, Amanda asked, "Have you found out anything yet?"

He shook his head wearily.

"Laura was in so much pain, and I couldn't do anything to help her, except hold her hand."

"That was probably the best thing you could have done." She hugged him, at the same time praying Nonnie would be all right. If it turned out to be serious, she'd never forgive herself. If she hadn't involved her grandmother in this harebrained scheme, Nonnie wouldn't have been out shopping and wouldn't have slipped on the ice.

An orderly wheeled Nonnie into the room as a nurse pulled the curtains back and said, "The doctor will be here shortly to explain the results of the x-rays." She took Nonnie's pulse, then left.

When the doctor arrived, he smiled at them encouragingly. "It's not as bad as we had anticipated. At first we thought the socket might be crushed and Mrs. Reynolds would need hip replacement surgery, but she lucked out."

The doctor turned back to Nonnie and patted her arm. "It's only a simple fracture. We'll get a cast on your leg and in no time at all, you'll be up running around."

"Just what I wanted to hear," she answered, a glimmer in her eyes. "I have a million things to do before Christmas."

Amanda was horrified. "Forget it, Nonnie," she ordered. "It's a good thing you haven't called Simon Kent yet."

"What makes you think I haven't?" she said, with a trace of her usual asperity. "I did, and he is thrilled to come. I won't let that poor man down."

"It's obviously out of the question now." Amanda's grandfather turned to her. "You'll have to call him and cancel."

Amanda agreed. "No publicity is worth Nonnie's health. Besides, what kind of person would come when his hostess has broken her leg?"

"That's just it," Nonnie said, her words slow with the exertion of speaking, "he won't—if he finds out. So he's not finding out! Amanda, you can just pretend to be me. I'll stay in the bedroom, and I can tell you what to do. He'll never even need to know I'm there."

"No!" Amanda's grandfather exploded. "Absolutely not!"

"Honestly, Nonnie," Amanda said with a smile. "I couldn't hoodwink someone like that." She rubbed her grandmother's cold hands as she spoke.

Nonnie gripped her hand so hard that it hurt. "You know how much Simon Kent has gone through.," she scolded. "You can't let him down. You can't let me down." She turned to her husband.

"Rob, you tell her."

He didn't look inclined to agree. "Sweetheart—" he began, but she cut him off.

"Rob, if you were ever taken hostage, or you"—she looked at Amanda—"I'd want to give you the best homecoming present it was in my power to give you. This fellow doesn't seem to have any family. Do you want him eating a TV dinner for Christmas?"

Amanda looked helplessly at her grandfather who shook his head at her. He knew what his wife was like when she got an idea in her head. Amanda felt her grandmother's grip losing its strength.

"We're ready to do your cast, Mrs. Reynolds," the nurse said cheerfully, coming to the side of the bed.

Nonnie's eyes held Amanda's until the nurse took her from the room. Amanda shook her head and sighed. "What am I going to do, Granddad?"

"You know how your grandmother is when she decides how things are going to be," her grandfather sympathized with her predicament. "She thinks Simon Kent deserves a special Christmas. You'll just have to do what she wants."

She stared at her grandfather in disbelief. "That's a little easier said than done," she protested. "I foresee several small problems, and I use the term *small* loosely. First of all, I don't cook, unless you count microwaving. Laura Reynolds *never* microwaves anything. Second, we're hardly the same age. If he's seen her picture, we're dead. Third—"

He held up his hand. "One at a time. As for your looks—you both have curly hair, and you've always been a younger version of Laura. He'll never notice the difference."

"So you think my condo can pass for Spindrift Farm?"

"Don't be silly." No one could express disgust as well as her grandfather. Amanda thought he must have perfected the look for myriads of lawyers, witnesses, and juries of the past. "Surely you know someone who owns a farm. And you're every bit as organized as Laura. You won't have any problems. In fact, you have an entire staff to help you."

"None of us, and I repeat, none of us, can come close to Nonnie's cooking. Without her food, the week will fail miserably."

"For heaven's sake, Laura has our house filled with Christmas food. Why don't you use it for Simon?"

Amanda felt herself losing the battle. "You know I'd do anything for Nonnie, but entertaining a stranger...and one who thinks he's being hosted by none other than Laura Reynolds..."

"You've been running that magazine for years now and that's no small accomplishment. There's no reason you can't give someone just as wonderful a Christmas as Laura could."

Amanda groaned silently. What a stupid idea this had been. If only she could move the clock back twenty-four hours. Now thanks to her, Nonnie had a broken leg, she herself was being recruited to masquerade as Laura Reynolds, and to top everything off, she was obviously going to miss St. Thomas this year.

Amanda found the nearest telephone and called a nursing service, learning that they needed twenty-four hours' notice. So she called a friend of a friend, who was a nurse, to see if she would stay with Nonnie or knew anyone who would (to her relief, she could!). Next, she took a taxi to pick up her grandfather's car and delivered it back to the hospital, then called her friend Nikki to pick up the nurse and take her to Charleston. She herself drove to her grandparents' home to get them settled, then drove back to Salt Lake, where she discovered a ticket on the windshield of her car. By the time she arrived back at her condo, it was midnight.

The end of a perfect day.

Chapter 3

Letter from Spindrift Farm—

*Part of the charm of Christmas is the press of things to do
as the day draws closer: the last minute shopping, the melody
of Silver Bells, a sense of eager anticipation filling the air,
and the good cheer of the crowds. I always like to plan ahead,
get everything organized, so I'm ready to improvise when
something unexpected happens.*

When the alarm rang at seven the next morning, Amanda's
eyelids felt like sandpaper, and only the sense of impending
doom sent her reeling from her bed to the shower. By the time
she turned off the water, she thought just possibly she might
make it through the day. However, she wasn't betting on it.

The first thing on her agenda was a phone call to her parents
in Switzerland about Nonnie's fall. Amanda thought they would
get a laugh out of the fact that she was impersonating Nonnie and
entertaining Simon Kent. She sighed. No St. Thomas this year.
Even when the whole charade was over it would be impossible to
book a room since it would be the height of the tourist season.

Her dad chuckled at her predicament, but he agreed with his
father-in-law that Laura would never rest as long as she believed
she had disappointed someone. The only thing Amanda could do
was host Simon Kent.

Her mother said they'd probably cancel St. Thomas for this year and come directly to Salt Lake so she could be with her dad and mother. "So we'll be seeing you between Christmas and New Year's, my Darling Girl."

Hearing her mother call her by her pet name, "Darling Girl," warmed Amanda and lifted her spirits. Her mother always inspired her with confidence that she could do anything. Exactly what she needed right now.

She called her grandparents and got the nurse who reported her grandmother had spent a restless night, but was sleeping now. By the time Amanda got to the office, Becki had arrived. Amanda informed her of Laura's accident and the change in plans which included a sudden need for a husband. As usual, her assistant was enthusiastic.

"The only real problem I foresee is Spindrift Farm— "

"Of course," Amanda interrupted in a scathing tone, her nerves raw. "Passing for Laura Reynolds is no problem. I'm only forty-five years younger."

"It's not like her face is that well known. She's never even been on TV," Becki brushed off her fears. "Do you really mean to tell me you're worried that someone will actually remember that picture on the cover of her book? How many copies did her book sell? Eighty thousand? We can estimate that a good half of them aren't *People* readers. It's simple." Becki smiled confidently, and added, "Just make sure Paul never gets a clear shot of your face."

Amanda rolled her eyes, but didn't say anything.

"The main problem is your condo. It just won't do. Laura Reynolds doesn't do manzanita branches strung with lights!"

Amanda leaned back in her leather chair. "The only person I know who owns a ranch is my dentist, and his family always spends Christmas there. What about you? Know anyone? You've got relatives everywhere!"

"Hey, I might know of one," she said slowly. "My brother has a farm in Idaho."

"Great!" Amanda responded warmly. At last, something was

going right. "Maybe his wife could do the cooking."

"Unfortunately not, they're staying with my parents. Jenny's expecting a baby anytime, and the doctor's here. Let me check with them." Becki hurried out. A few minutes later she returned, her face beaming. "Ben said he'd be glad to have someone in the house while they're gone. So that's settled. They also have a duck pond for ice-skating."

Amanda shook her head. "Don't even mention it." Then she had a brilliant idea. "Why don't you come with us?"

Becki's face drooped in obvious disappointment. "Gee, I'm sorry, Amanda, but I've made plans I don't think I can get out of."

Amanda's uneasiness returned, but she did her best to shake it off. "Well, then, get me a copy of the December issue."

Carefully going through the column, Amanda underlined all the things she would have to do to make the week work. It should be simple enough. Of course, Nonnie always made things look simple. And Amanda was fond of saying that if a person could read, she could do anything. Now her own words came back to haunt her. She crossed her fingers. She turned to the recipes. They didn't sound too hard, and it wasn't as if she'd never used a stove before.

Becki called the Marshall Talent Agency for someone to play the part of Laura's husband, Rob. *Maybe he can cook*, Amanda thought to herself wryly. *Laura Reynolds's secret weapon.*

Now all she had to do was call Simon Kent, plus a hundred more little things, and she'd be ready. This thought had no more than crossed her mind when Becki informed her that Simon Kent was on the line. She cleared her throat and tried to speak in a deeper voice than usual so he wouldn't recognize it when they finally met.

"Hello, Mr. Kent. This is Amanda Richards, editor of *Today's Home.* How are you today?"

"Fine." His voice was a warm, rich baritone. "Glad to be in Utah. I can't wait to try out the powder."

Amanda was puzzled. Skiing at his age?

"By the way," he continued, "I enjoyed your magazine. Laura Reynolds sure knows how to celebrate Christmas. I can hardly wait."

"I'm calling to finalize our plans." She hoped he'd go for the publicity. "We'd like to send a photographer and do an article about your week with Laura for our magazine. It may even be in *People* magazine too. After what you've been through, you deserve a wonderful celebration."

"I don't know about that, but I am anxious to come. A photographer is the least of my worries."

Amanda relaxed. At least she wouldn't be cooking in vain. They'd get some publicity for the magazine out of this week.

He continued, "You wanted me on the eighteenth? I need to be back here on the twenty-sixth. I just received word my brother will be arriving then from Hong Kong."

The eighteenth? Amanda blanched. That gave them two days to get ready. She forced herself to say, "That will be great!" Why on earth had Nonnie invited him so soon? She could imagine Nonnie saying cheerfully, "Of course, you can join in our pre-Christmas festivities."

"Terrific." His voice had a boyish enthusiasm that Amanda found charming for someone his age. "Where is Spindrift Farm?"

"In Idaho." Beyond that vague direction she had no idea. "Would you like to ride up with us?" She was sure Paul Merritt would give him a lift. She, herself, planned to be safely entrenched at the farm with every little detail in place.

"I've rented a car, so I'll just drive up."

Rented a car? Someone Mr. Kent's age had no business driving that far alone during the winter. But old people tended to be sensitive about driving—as her granddad had been last night. Although he'd insisted on driving, Amanda's sheer persistence had finally worn him down. Remembering the fight her grandfather had put up, Amanda said nothing to her guest-to-be.

"How do I get there?"

Thinking fast, she said, "I'll fax a map to the hotel."

When she finally said good-bye, Amanda felt drained. If she didn't do it, Granddad and Nonnie would never forgive her; on the other hand, if she did...if she could...? No, she had no faith in her ability to pull this scam off. But there was no way she could cancel the visit. The genuine happiness in Mr. Kent's voice made that obvious.

She stood up and stretched the kinks out of her back. Only two days. *Organization is the key*, she told herself grimly.

"He agreed to the photographer?" Becki sounded as eager as Simon Kent.

"Yes."

"Fantastic! Our readers will love the fact that we've granted Simon Kent's wish. We'll revive all their memories of Christmases past. It will make Laura Reynolds come alive for them and cement them to us for years to come." Now Becki's business side came to the fore. She worried about circulation even more than Amanda did. A little more experience on top of her business drive, and Becki would be ready for a promotion.

Amanda remembered all the little details of Laura Reynolds's Christmas column, and as the images built in her mind, panic grew in the pit of her stomach. She took a deep breath. Why was she so tense? This would be a piece of cake, figuratively, if not literally. All it took was planning. She grimaced. Who was she trying to kid? She was a lousy cook. Thank heavens for Nonnie's goodies! They should help.

Becki held out a list. "I've talked to Denise at the Marshall Agency, and she's sending over a couple of actors this afternoon. And I've made a list of all the supplies you'll need. Now what?"

Amanda took a deep breath to calm herself. "Get the editor at *People* while I go over the list. We've only got two days. I want to get up there on the seventeenth, so I'll have a day to get organized before Simon Kent arrives. Can you believe it? He insisted on driving himself. He's sixty if he's a day!"

As her eyes took in the list, Amanda was filled with doubts.

She'd so looked forward to spending the nineteenth—her first full day in St. Thomas—lying on the beach, soaking up the sun, catching up on all the news with her parents. Instead she'd be stuck in Idaho—rural Idaho, no less!—pretending to be the nation's foremost authority on country living. All because she'd wanted more readers.

By the time she was ready to leave for the day, she'd sold *People* on a two-page spread and she'd hired a blond cowboy type to play Rob, her husband. She had also plotted every hour of the next week, leaving nothing to chance. Her careful plans gave her a feeling of satisfaction. If there were no slip-ups, she'd be home free.

On Thursday, she drove to Charleston to check on her grandparents and to pick up the cookies and gingerbread from their kitchen. She learned that Nonnie wasn't in much pain, for which Amanda was grateful. Granddad and Nonnie also raved about the new nurse. Not only was she young and bubbly, but she also played the piano. Laura sighed. So much for a medical background!

It was nearly three o'clock by the time she left her condominium in the Avenues to finish running her errands. First stop, the florist. She hoped everything she'd ordered would be boxed and ready to go. Wreaths, garlands, mistletoe, and holly. Then on to the display store for lights, tree decorations, and plenty of red velvet ribbon for bows.

The food editor had picked up fruitcake, dried fruit, along with mincemeat in plain jars from The Silver Spoon. The art department had finished some "From the Kitchen of Laura Reynolds" labels for her.

Since Utah residents eat more pounds of candy per capita than people in any other place in the world, Amanda had no problem finding hand-dipped chocolates. She assigned Becki to locate chestnuts for the dressing, which turned out to be the toughest errand of all. After calling six supermarkets, Becki finally found some. Amanda was grateful Nonnie hadn't put fresh roast goose on her menu.

Next some Christmas gifts—a bright blue sweater for Rob, a sensible gray one for Simon Kent, and a wheel of imported cheeses for Paul. For herself, thermal underwear, a purchase she'd never dreamed she would ever need.

Even with Becki's help, the preparations ended up taking hours. Back at the magazine offices, Amanda collected what she needed and Becki took the rest to load in Paul's car.

By the time Amanda finally staggered into her condo for the last time, light snow flurries were dancing in the car lights and dusting the sidewalks.

As she walked through her front door, the telephone was ringing. It was her father, calling to tell her they'd be arriving on the nineteenth. Before he hung up, he chuckled at her predicament. "Remember, 'She who lives by the pen, dies by the pen.'" Amanda shuddered. A thought only too true—this next week might be the death of her.

She slipped out of her coat, brushing the melted flakes of snow from her hair and turning on the television. The forecast called for a mild storm with light winds and only a ten percent chance of significant snow during the night. Thank goodness! Even with her new snow tires, she hated driving on snow-packed roads.

After a restless night, Amanda woke to the jarring ring of the phone. Half asleep, she rolled over, knocked the receiver onto the floor, struggled to find the switch on the lamp, and eventually reeled in the phone with its cord.

"Mmmm?"

"Amanda? Are you there? Are you awake?"

"Becki?"

"I was hoping to catch you before you left."

Immediately her heart sank. What had gone wrong? "Why?" Her bleary eyes focused on the lighted dial of the alarm, and she saw that it was only seven.

"We've had a change in plans."

"Oh, no!"

"The actor has to finish a commercial this morning and won't be able to leave until noon. I've taken care of my commitments, so I can come—if you still want me."

"Need you ask?" For some reason Amanda found hard to define—Becki cooked no better than she did—her words gave her a feeling of relief.

"I'm so excited about this," Becki bubbled. "We're going to show that poor man the time of his life. I love being in the wish-granting business."

"Just be sure you get there as soon as possible. I don't want to be alone in that house one minute longer than necessary."

"It's only a five-hour drive. We'll be there by supper."

"I'm counting on it." The last two days had been exhausting, but with everything on the list checked and double checked, she was confident nothing could go wrong.

"Don't worry about unpacking. We'll help you when we get there. Jenny says to make yourself at home. Ciao."

Wearily Amanda threw back the covers and stumbled toward the window. Outside, it was still dark, but it looked like the storm had only dampened the streets. She put a couple of frozen croissants into the oven and headed for the shower. Everything she'd need for the week was packed, the clothes she intended to wear set out on the bed, the boxes and coolers ready to be loaded into her car. In the rush of the last two days, she hadn't given Becki her Christmas gift, so she put it on top of the boxes. She certainly deserved a bigger gift, but for now the handmade ornament would have to suffice.

Just before nine, Amanda pulled into the stream of traffic heading north out of Salt Lake. By the time she reached Brigham City it was snowing. She turned on the radio station just in time to hear that a blizzard was now on its way. Just her luck. Why couldn't it have been a couple of days sooner? The weather bureau warned that by evening travelers' advisories would be in effect.

When she reached Logan Canyon, the snow had become

heavier; several inches had already accumulated on the roads. On Highway 89 through Wyoming, progress slowed to twenty miles an hour with visibility nearly zero. By mid-afternoon she had crossed the border into Idaho, her shoulders and neck aching from her fight with the storm. All she wanted was a hot bath and a warm bed.

When she finally turned onto Highway 26, Amanda found the state road had been plowed, but several more inches had already fallen. She gripped the wheel nervously. Why hadn't she rented a four-wheel drive vehicle?

She passed through Swan Valley with a mixed sense of relief and accomplishment. Now the farm was only four miles away. Creeping along at a snail's pace, she held Becki's hand-drawn map in her lap and drove with the dome light on, watching for landmarks through the blowing, drifting snow.

Amanda glanced frequently at the odometer, counting each slow number change until she'd gone exactly four miles. Coming to almost a complete stop, she peered through the falling snow. Not a building in sight. She barely saw the sign indicating that she was nearly at the Canfield farm. She stepped on the brake and the back wheels skidded toward the right. Panic tightened her throat as she straightened the car and edged into the lane. Afraid she might get stuck, she increased the pressure of her foot on the accelerator, and the car fishtailed again. She twisted the wheel, but the rear end continued to slide. And slide. With a jolt, it stopped, its offside wheels in the ditch. Her heart pounding, Amanda sat for a minute to steady her ragged breathing. She pressed the gas pedal hopefully, but the wheels only spun in the snow.

Well, at least she wasn't lost. According to the map the house had to be up this lane. She reached for her snow boots, stashed conveniently on the floor next to her, and struggled into them. Then she attempted to stuff her crimped hair into a knit cap. Failing to do that, she pulled the cap down, letting her long hair hang free down her back. It had been an endless, miserable, tiring, stressful day. With a determined straightening of her shoulders, she unlocked the car door and tried to push it open.

But the snow drift caught at it, holding the door back, and Amanda realized she wasn't home free. Pushing it open as far as she could, she squeezed through the hard-earned eight inches and stepped into the bank. It was deeper than her boot, which immediately filled with snow.

What a ridiculous idea this had been. Suddenly angry with her grandparents and herself for thinking it would work, Amanda reached back into the car and jerked her suitcase off the seat. She forced it through the opening, slammed the car door and turned determinedly up the lane. Snow and cold and wet feet notwithstanding, she wouldn't let them or this situation defeat her.

Slipping and sliding, she made it out of the gully and onto the lane. She shivered. Just what she hated—snow and cold. She shivered again. The wind was starting to pick up. She gritted her teeth as she slogged another foot through the snow. Maybe trying to make the house was stupid. What if she got lost? She could see the headlines now. "Editor Perishes in Blizzard" with a sub heading, "Doing her Good Deed" or if they were mean-spirited, "Desperate for Publicity."

The wisest thing would be to return to the car. She stopped to survey both sides of the lane again. This time she saw a dark shadow looming through the trees. She gasped her relief. It had to be the house. It took ten minutes to conquer the remaining distance, and every step seemed preprogrammed to drain away her energy. When she finally clumped up the steps she felt frozen to the bone, and her fingers fumbled with the key Becki had provided.

The large entrance hall was dark and dank, and she could barely make out an imposing staircase going to the second floor. To her right, double pocket doors opened to the living room. The air was stuffy, as if no one had lived there for months; the Canfields, she knew, had only been in town a couple of weeks. The house needed airing, but Amanda needed warmth more. She pulled off her cap and shook her head in an effort to shake off the snow still clinging to her hair. Yanking off her gloves, she rubbed her hands to renew the circulation. Then moving from room to room, turning on lights as she went to orient herself, she looked for the thermostat. Though not decorated to Amanda's taste, the living room looked like something Nonnie would love. Its pine furniture, calico prints, and braided rag rugs were charming. A fire in the fireplace and good smells coming from the kitchen would make it cozy and inviting. Tonight it just seemed foreign and lonely. And cold. The den had probably originally been the parlor. But without a fire in the fireplace it seemed cheerless. A large oak table dominated the small dining room. An ornate antique lamp had been wired for electricity and hung over the table.

When she couldn't find the thermostat, prickles of dread made her feel still colder. Surely in this day and age no one would live without the amenities of life and, in her book, central heating was at the top of the list. Relief flooded her when she finally noticed the heat vents.

The kitchen was as homey as the living and dining rooms. Paper with small blue lovebirds and rose-colored hearts covered the walls. Prints of Early American scenes hung on one wall, while hearts from various materials and of different sizes were attractively grouped over a small kitchen table. Then her eyes lit on the huge Monarch wood range. Oh, no! Nonnie had written about the virtues of wood-burning ranges—she'd even owned one once. But why couldn't Jennie and Ben use something more modern? And why hadn't Becki warned her that this would be a week of roughing it?

Thank heavens she can come after all, Amanda consoled herself. *She can take over.* Suddenly another possibility occurred to her. What if there were no hot water? She hurried to the sink and turned the tap. It took nearly a minute, but the water gradually grew warmer. The house might be cold, her car stuck in a ditch, and the stove a nightmare, but at least she could have a nice hot bath! She smiled in anticipation and picked up the suitcase.

She had just started up the stairs when a sudden, heavy pounding at the door stopped her. The sound came so abruptly that her heart jerked in her chest, and she leaned against the wall, grasping at reason to still the panic. Becki! Relieved, she dropped her suitcase, took a deep breath to release the last of the fear, and hurried to fling open the door.

"Am I gl—" The rest stuck in her throat. It wasn't Becki. In the pale slanting light from inside the house, only impressions of the stranger at her door registered in her mind. He was tall and lean, in his late thirties, and his eyes were deep and penetrating, as if he saw beyond the surface of things.

"I'm looking for Spindrift Farm."

Amanda stared at him for a moment unable to comprehend his words. "Spindrift Farm?" she sputtered, stunned.

The stranger looked at her as if she had taken leave of her senses. "Can you tell me how to find it?"

And she'd imagined nothing else could go wrong.

"You're not Simon Kent?"

Chapter 4

Letter from Spindrift Farm—

This is one of the most joyful times of year—a time for the uniting of scattered friends and family. We never know who might show up, and that's one of the delights—unexpected company. As in colonial times, our latch string is always out.

"Yes. I'm Simon Kent." He looked puzzled for a moment, and then an expression of astonishment flickered across his face. "You're not Laura Reynolds?"

"Yes." Amanda smothered a groan, wondering what she should do next.

He hesitated before saying, apologetically, "I know I'm early. But when I heard the weather report, I was afraid the storm might keep me away if I waited."

"I'm glad you came today." Liar. Right now she wished he'd gotten snowed in at Park City, so they could have both missed this experience entirely. "We wanted you to help with all the preparations." Amanda pushed the door open wider. "Please come in. But I'm afraid it's not much warmer inside."

He stamped the snow off his feet and brushed it off his coat sleeves, but his eyes kept finding their way back to Amanda. Uncomfortable in his perusal, she stepped aside, holding the door for him. How had she gotten the impression Simon Kent was old? Or grizzled, or unfortunate? Or would look good in a serviceable gray sweater?

Simon Kent was closer to thirty-five than sixty-five, as well as clean-shaven, lean, and tall. Although he wore a tan shearling parka, it looked well-cut and expensive. His dark windblown hair was streaked with gray, distinguished and debonair. His eyes were midnight blue and fathomless.

Shutting the door, she nearly brushed against him. She stepped back nervously, thinking that if she could just be any-where but here right now, she'd even settle for the North Pole. Then his deep voice brought her back to reality.

"Excuse me for staring. But who takes your publicity pictures? From the back cover of your book, I was expecting someone more..." *Someone more homey and grandmotherly*, he thought in surprise. Not someone only four or five years younger than him-self. Not someone with long, streaked blond hair that waved invitingly around her face. Not someone wearing designer jeans. Not someone who looked like they wouldn't know the working end of a can opener from the other.

He couldn't seem to quit staring. Never in his wildest dreams had he expected someone like her. So young and vital.

"Well, I might ask you the same thing," she said with a touch of sharpness. "I was expecting Rip Van Winkle."

He laughed. How ironic. She was as shocked as he was. "It's wonderful what a few days in San Francisco will do. A shave, a haircut, and some decent-fitting clothes."

Amanda frowned in consternation. This man oozed sophisti-cated assurance. Why would he want a countrified Christmas when he looked as if he liked life in the fast lane? She glanced at the snowflakes glistening on the silvered strands of mahogany hair. Her eyes traveled downward to the tanned face. The lines etched around his eyes and on either side of his mouth spoke of laughter, but most of all they seemed to speak of a life that hadn't always been easy.

There was an alertness in his eyes that she would do well to acknowledge from the start if she had any hope of carrying off this week. He had a fundamental strength, a self-confidence that she recognized immediately. Her senses reacted to that unconscious force while she absorbed his features—the taut, lean planes of his jaw and chin, the firmness of his mouth, and most of all the quiet authority with which he stood facing her.

Amanda looked at his lips again, curving into a quizzical smile, and with a start she realized she'd been staring.

She held out her hand. "Here, let me take your coat. I'm afraid I just got here myself, but my...uh—husband and the others should be arriving anytime. We have a place in Salt Lake City and spend about half our time there. So if the house smells a little musty to you, it's because we've been gone." The words just tripped off her tongue. At this rate, she should have been a fiction writer.

He handed her his coat, then shivered slightly in the chill. The house was colder than he had expected and also had an unlived-in quality, probably because they hadn't been here for a while. But why invite him if they weren't living here?

"Maybe you'd rather keep it until I get the heat turned up." The words came easily, but Amanda still didn't know where the thermostat was.

"No, I'm fine, really."

She turned toward the nearest door, then realized it might not be the closet. Silently muttering something between an oath and a prayer, she pulled open the door and breathed a sigh of thanks when, this time, fate was in her favor.

"Most of our Christmas things are out in my car," she said over her shoulder. "Maybe you saw it when you came up the lane. I skidded into the ditch."

"Yes, I did. I wondered about it. Are you all right?"

"Oh, sure. I was only going about a half mile an hour." The warm concern in his voice didn't allay the alarm she felt over his early arrival.

"Just the way I envisioned it," he said as he followed her into the living room.

"I'm glad it's living up to your expectations." Was she ever! What on earth was she going to do now? She hadn't planned on ever being alone with him. Having the others here while she stage-managed the affair was one thing, but winging it alone was something else again.

Before she could say anything more, Amanda heard a phone ring faintly in the distance. Acting as if she knew exactly what she was doing, she casually went into the dining room, trying to follow the sound. When she pushed open the kitchen door, the ring was louder, and she found the phone hanging behind the door.

"Amanda? Thank goodness you finally got there. Is it snowing?"

Becki. Why couldn't she have been at the door instead of on the phone. "Only a blizzard. Are you calling from near here?"

In her usual cheery voice, Becki said, "We have a small problem. Just after you left, the storm hit Salt Lake full force. Guess what? We're marooned here until the roads are opened, but that's—"

"Marooned!" Amanda nearly yelled. Then she lowered her voice to a whisper, "He's here!"

"Who?"

"Who do you think? Simon Kent!"

"Simon Kent? He's not coming until tomorrow."

"You know that, I know that, but he doesn't. And do you have any idea how old he is?"

"Late sixties, early seventies."

"Wrong! More like late thirties, early forties." When Becki made no reply, Amanda continued. "What am I going to do for food?"

"Check the pantry. You'll also find a well-stocked freezer on the back porch. Ben and his wife are one couple that has their year's supply. Use what you need. They won't mind as long as we replace it."

"Why didn't you mention the stove?" Amanda whispered furiously.

"The stove? Oh, no. I'm so used to it, I forgot all about it. Don't worry. Jenny doesn't seem to have any trouble. It must be simple. You'll manage just fine."

"Easy enough for you to say. You're not on the front lines trying to demonstrate gracious country living." Amanda didn't attempt to hide her frustration. "What a mess! Snowed in with a stranger in an isolated farmhouse. I hope he doesn't turn out to be an axe-murderer. Something tells me this entire idea is ill-fated."

"Just hang on until we get there. Paul says he'll see you as soon as the roads are plowed, which should be tomorrow."

Before she could ask Becki about the heat, the line went dead. Banging up the receiver, Amanda unenthusiastically returned to the living room where she found her guest staring out the window.

He turned, and smiling ruefully, said, "Look, I know you weren't expecting me until tomorrow, and I really don't want to put you to any unnecessary effort. How about if I start a fire, and you can do whatever else you need to do?"

Rescued. At least temporarily. "That would be great." With the neat stack of wood in the firebox he shouldn't have too much difficulty. "My husband just called, and they are stranded in town until this lets up. So I guess we're on our own." She crossed her fingers. "For tonight anyway."

His smile changed to one of sympathy. "That's too bad. I guess we're just lucky we made it."

"True." He might say that, but she had other words to describe it! Leaving the fire to him, she checked the dining room again for the thermostat. She heaved a sigh of relief when she found it nearly hidden by a picture made of pressed flowers. After turning up the heat, she hurried upstairs to check out the bedrooms.

All the doors in the hallway were shut, so Amanda opened and closed each of them as softly as she could. There were four bedrooms, and two baths, one accessible only through the master bedroom, which was located at the back, next to a flight of stairs. She ran up them and discovered an unfinished attic. This was going to be tricky. Unless there was another bedroom downstairs that she hadn't found, someone was going to have to share. And it couldn't be Becki and her because she had to act like Rob shared her room.

Outside the wind whistled and moaned, rattling the shutters and making the trees thrash together in response. Amanda glanced at her watch and saw in dismay that it was only 6:30. Deciding to give Simon Kent the room farthest from the master bedroom, she turned down the covers and plumped up the pillows. There, that ought to make him feel welcome.

She found him crouched before the fireplace with his back to her. His wool flannel shirt fit snugly, showing a lean frame without a spare ounce of fat. Obviously, he hadn't spent his time in captivity eating. He must have heard her come in, because he turned and smiled. "There." He indicated the growing blaze with a grin that tickled a response somewhere in Amanda's midsection. No, this man was definitely not Rip Van Winkle.

"After the day I've spent, this is marvelous," Amanda said, appreciating the warmth.

"I know what you mean. Driving in snow isn't like riding a bicycle—you do forget how to do it."

"Yes. I haven't driven—" she stopped abruptly, her heart skipping a beat. Someone who lived in this remote place couldn't admit she seldom drove in snow. Amanda rubbed her neck trying to think of how to correct her mistake. "There's nothing like slick roads and a death grip on the steering wheel to make your muscles tense up." Saved. "If your shoulders are as tight as mine, maybe you'd like to take a hot shower. Your room's on the right at the top of the stairs, and the bathroom's next to it. In the meantime, I can fix us something to eat. If you were racing the storm, you probably didn't stop."

"No, I didn't. And I'll bet you didn't either, if you got in just before I did."

With a light laugh, she agreed. "No, and I'm starving."

"I think the shower can wait. But I will take my suitcase up and check out the quarters, then I'll come back and help you."

"Oh, you just go ahead and relax. You're a guest of Laura Reynolds now." In name only! The last thing Amanda needed was to have him watching over her shoulder while she tried to find things. She didn't even know if there was any food in the kitchen that wasn't frozen. She might have to tramp out to the car and bring in some of Nonnie's Christmas goodies just to keep starvation at bay. She wondered how he'd feel about sugar cookies and mincemeat for supper.

Once in the kitchen, she quickly checked the cupboards and drawers to familiarize herself with where things were. When she opened the pantry door she stared in amazement. Row after row of Mason jars filled with fruits and vegetables lined the shelves, as if they were jewels stored carefully away. The amber of peaches, the ruby of cherries, the opalescence of pears. String beans, carrots, beets and rhubarb. Applesauce and maple syrup. Jenny not only had a year's supply, she'd bottled it all herself! Amanda knew she'd have a hard time opening any of them when it was so easy to imagine the hours of work that went into such an effort. But she knew Simon Kent would love this example of homeliness. Just for him she might open a couple of bottles. She'd pay Jenny for them, even send her a subscription to *Today's Home*, though it was hardly fair compensation for her labor.

Thankfully, shelves along the opposite wall held a selection, albeit sparse, of commercially canned goods, and those she could replace. Amanda looked at the Monarch stove and tentatively lifted the cast-iron plate on the range top. She had read about wood-burning stoves in Nonnie's column, but this was the first time she'd ever seen one in real life.

"I know you're used to it, but let me do that."

At the sound of Simon Kent's voice, she jumped and dropped the plate, turning abruptly to face him. "What makes you think I'm used to it?"

"Your column," he replied with a smile. "You said how much you enjoyed an old-fashioned wood range. How much it added to the warmth of the kitchen." He studied the room with interest. "Is this where you test your recipes for your column?"

"Uh—h." She glanced around the kitchen, feeling trapped. No matter what she answered, she felt that the consequences could be perilous. Finally, deciding on honesty, she said, "No. They're perfected in the test kitchen"—Nonnie's—"and then I try them here." Like tomorrow and the rest of the week.

She gave him a cheerful friendly smile, although the effort to force her muscles into that position was almost more than she could endure. "Do you mind making another fire?"

"No." Simon flashed Laura a self-confident grin, hoping to ease his guilt feelings at arriving a day early. He couldn't put his finger on it, but something wasn't right. There was a nervous tension in the air, as if she didn't quite know what to do. But that couldn't be it. He knew from her book *Harvest Time at Spindrift Farm* that she was an expert on rural living. Maybe her nervousness was the result of being alone with a stranger. "You may be Laura Reynolds, but even so, I don't feel comfortable letting you do all the work."

"You know how this works?" Amanda touched the stove and hardly dared breathe as she waited for his answer.

"Sure. My grandmother had one. Since she didn't believe in incompetence, I was a master by the time I was ten."

Feeling more confident with one more obstacle out of the way, she said, "Then by all means, be my guest. You handle the stove, and I'll handle the food."

He rested one palm on the cold stove and looked down at her with a twinkle in his deep, dark eyes. "I can hardly wait to see what Laura Reynolds whips up for dinner on a cold stormy night."

Amanda could hardly wait herself. She selectively visualized the contents of the pantry. "Since my husband was stopping at the store on his way," she improvised, "how does Campbell's

Soup sound?"

"Wonderful. Jazzed up the way you described in *Harvest Time at Spindrift Farm*?" he said, going into the living room and coming back with wood and newspapers.

With an inward groan, she pasted a smile of delight on her face. "You've read my book!"

"Of course. I went out and bought it the minute I hung up from talking to you."

Lowering her voice conspiratorially, Amanda winked at him. "Even Laura Reynolds takes a night off, especially on a cold stormy night when the cupboard is bare. I thought we'd just open a can."

"At this point, just being here is enough. Now, where are the matches?" Without waiting for an answer, he reached onto the warming oven and found them. "Just where my grandmother hid hers." The next minute he had the fire going.

"Some things are just too obvious to change," Amanda said, wondering how long it would have taken her to think to look there. Returning to the pantry, she almost wished she could fix something special for him. He'd been understanding and helpful, and even under the circumstances, he deserved better than canned soup. With a heavy sigh, she counted off the items on the shelves. Tomato, cream of mushroom, chicken and rice soups, chicken bouillon. Next shelf down, pineapple, canned milk, pumpkin. She bent closer to see what the large tin on the floor contained. Cocoa mix. Now that was something she was an expert at: adding hot water to cocoa mix.

She looked at the shelves again, and her eyes lit on the pumpkin. Pumpkin! Nonnie had included a recipe for pumpkin soup in her book, and Amanda could vaguely remember the ingredients, if not the precise amounts. She crossed her fingers, hoping against hope that the Canfields had what she needed. Otherwise she'd improvise. Good cooks always improvised, though not by any stretch of the imagination could she be considered a good cook. Eagerly she grabbed up the pumpkin, chicken bouillon, and canned milk, then checked the spice shelves for onion salt and cloves. In the nearly empty refrigerator she found lemon juice, but no Tabasco sauce; however, on the bottom shelf of the door was a half-filled bottle of what looked like taco sauce. She'd substitute.

"Just wait. You're in for the taste treat of the decade." She found a soup pot in the cupboard next to the stove and deftly stirred up the ingredients as if it were something she did every day. Was taco sauce as hot as Tabasco? She doubted it, so she emptied in the entire bottle. Simon leaned one hip against the cupboard and watched. "Hey, I think I recognize this. It's your pumpkin soup!"

"Well, when it came right down to it, I just had to live up to Laura Reynolds's reputation." After stirring the soup briskly a couple of times, Amanda sampled the concoction to see what other seasonings it might need.

"Not too bad—" then as if the soup had been acid, it started burning, strangling her, and she started coughing. She dropped the spoon and held her throat. "Water," she whispered, between coughs, tears running down her face.

Startled, Simon quickly found a glass and filled it. Amanda took a big swallow, only to find that the water didn't help at all; it only triggered more coughing. Slumping against the counter, she tried to control her coughing and waited for the burning to subside. What had been in that bottle? They should have labeled it poison or lethal weapon. Another thought struck her. How did she explain this to Simon Kent?

"I take it the soup was too hot." Simon hovered over her still looking worried. "Are you all right?"

"Yes." But the soft, whispery sound of Amanda's voice didn't sound all right, and what she wanted to do was sit down and wait for her strength to return. But what would Laura Reynolds do? "Let me get some more pumpkin and start over. This time I'll just add a couple of spoonfuls of the original soup to it." She managed a smile. "I know for sure that'll give it a zing."

Simon held up his hand to protest. "Campbell's will do."

"Since I've just had the taste treat of the decade, I'm willing to settle for something a little less exotic myself. I can't imagine what Rob had in that bottle." She had to blame someone, and Rob was a perfect choice.

Simon stirred through the pumpkin soup. "It looks like yellow chili peppers."

"Yellow chili peppers?" Why hadn't she noticed the taco sauce wasn't red? She knew why. Too busy being "Marvelous Laura Reynolds" to pay attention to what she was doing. "Just wait, I'll get even!" She ducked into the pantry. "What do you want? Tomato or chicken and rice?" So much for Laura Reynolds's reputation. Much more innovation and there would be none left.

"Tomato," he said simply.

Amanda opened the can, added canned milk and water, stirring it well. Then as if this were an everyday occurrence, she unlocked the back door. Stepping outside, she found a glassed-in porch that seemed to stretch along the entire rear of the house. There nestled between stacks of firewood was the freezer. If Jenny froze food the way she canned, surely there would be something to go along with the soup. When she lifted the freezer lid, she wasn't disappointed. Chicken, frozen berries, and underneath the jam lay several pies. And loaves and loaves of bread. One thing even Amanda Richards knew was how to toast bread in a Monarch cooking range. "Thank you, Jenny," she whispered fervently.

Her arms loaded, Amanda returned to the kitchen. "There's plenty of firewood on the porch." Suddenly, fiercely, a more violent gust of wind hammered at the house, rattling the windows.

"Not a good night to be outside," Simon said pensively. He lifted one of the cast iron plates on the stove, poked the fire through the hole, then placed the pan of soup on the plate. "Thanks for not objecting to my early arrival."

Laughing lightly, she unwrapped the pie which turned out to

be apple. "Well, it is a terrible imposition. I would have turned you away, but on nights like this I prefer not to be alone in the house." Finding a knife with a serrated edge, she sawed through the frozen bread.

Simon stared at her curiously. "What does your husband do? I thought you both ran the farm and that you wrote your column on the side."

A totally reasonable question except that Amanda didn't know how to explain how Laura's husband would be old enough to be a retired lawyer. So what could she create for Rob to do that would keep him around here? Rashly, she said the first thing that came to her mind.

"Rob's a writer, too." She crossed her fingers that the actor knew something about writing.

"How interesting. That would give you a lot in common. What does he write?"

"Uh—h…Westerns." Hoping to keep from getting in any deeper, she added, "The farm is our first love, but during the winter when the snow keeps us indoors, he likes to exercise his imagination."

"Westerns, huh? What's he written? Every once in a while I read a Louis L'Amour."

Amanda stifled the need for a deep, nerve-calming breath and shook her head. "He's just completed his first one."

Simon looked at her expectantly.

"Uh… which won't be out until late—" when he continued looking at her, she felt compelled to say something more "—next year. That's why he had to stay in town… to finish rewrites… so he could express them to New York."

Simon nodded and turned back to stir the soup again. "Well, you'll have to let me know when it comes out so I can read it."

"Oh, we will." And she hoped she'd have a chance to tell the actor that he had two professions before he blew it. As of two minutes ago, he was a writer as well as a farmer.

"I'm looking forward to meeting him."

"He's looking forward to meeting you, too." Especially since it was a paid acting job and paid acting jobs in Salt Lake weren't easy to come by.

Simon leaned over and stirred the soup, taking a deep breath. "This smells delicious."

Amanda smiled. "You are hungry. This frozen bread will take about ten minutes to heat, if the oven's hot enough." Placing the bread on a pie tin she found in the cupboard, she slid it into the oven. "Why don't we eat in front of the fire in the living room. Do you mind sitting on the floor?"

He laughed at that. And his laugh rumbled around her, tugging at her emotions, reminding her of distant days when joking around with her father was part of the daily ritual. "I'm very good at sitting on floors, or tree stumps, or rocks."

"Well, at least this floor isn't dirt."

"That," he agreed, "is a major attraction."

A few minutes later, after putting the pie in the oven, Simon followed Amanda into the living room, carefully carrying a tray loaded with hot bread and mugs of soup.

"If you like, we can pull the couch over closer," Amanda offered.

He grinned mischievously at her. "Personally, I have nothing against the floor."

"The floor it is then."

He tasted the soup first and then the bread, before letting out a contented sigh. "This is wonderful. I don't think I've tasted anything better since I got home."

"It does taste good, doesn't it?" She couldn't help the surprised tone in her voice. Even though she fixed canned soup often and found it nourishing and filling, she seldom thought of it as tasty.

Only the sound of wind-driven snow lashing against the house broke the silence. Finally, Amanda said, "The storm is much worse than anybody expected, isn't it, coming in so fast that they had to close the roads?"

"I guess the snow's simply too heavy for them to keep up.

41

Especially with the wind blowing this hard."

"On nights like this, I'm always glad to be inside." She turned her attention to her companion. The fire made shadows dance on his face, lighting it, then casting it into shadows, making him seem mysterious and intriguing. His dark eyes seemed to smolder. If she were playing Amanda Richards instead of Laura Reynolds, she would find being snowbound with Simon Kent extremely enjoyable. She sighed.

"So much for a ten percent chance and light winds. Are you worried about your husband's making it home?"

"If the weather doesn't let up, who knows when they'll get out of the city. Listen," Amanda said suddenly, turning toward him and wrapping her arms around her knees. "There's no point in my sitting here worrying about things I can't change. Would it be impolite of me to ask you about yourself? What's your family like? You were going to spend Christmas skiing with them?"

"No. My only brother John is in Hong Kong and can't get away until the first of the year. We're both in banking and usually work in opposite corners of the world. My parents are no longer living, so ordinarily we spend the holidays together, skiing in Utah. He's married and has two kids, a boy and a girl.

"I'm surprised that someone who travels as much as you have would find tradition important." The idea seemed inconceivable to her.

The tone of her voice surprised him. She sounded so skeptical. He glanced at her again. "It hasn't always been. One of the things I liked best about my job was the constant change—meeting new people, learning new customs. But after months as the unwilling house guest of rebels, tradition has started to look better and better."

The wind had died for a moment, the room was quiet, and the mood between them mellow. At last, reluctantly, Amanda placed her dishes on the tray and reached for his. "Here, let me take these to the kitchen." She checked the pie and found it browned and bubbly, so she removed it from the oven.

When she came back into the living room, Simon stood with his back to the fire.

"Shall we have our pie now or later?"

"After all that hot bread, I'd just as soon wait. You said your things are still out in your car. Does any of it need to come in tonight?"

She hesitated a moment. "Probably. Nothing can spoil in this cold, but freezing might harm some of it."

"Okay, let me get my coat." He started towards the hall, but she came after him, touching his arm before he even reached the door.

"Wait, do you have boots? I can't let you go out in this."

"They're in my car." Simon looked down into Amanda's bright green eyes which were smiling back at him. "I came prepared for anything." He took the stairs two at a time. When he came back down, she had her coat and boots on, and a blue and white knit cap pulled down snugly around her face and matching blue and white gloves.

"I couldn't find a flashlight," Amanda tried to speak lightly. "Rob must have used it for something and not put it back. Do you think it'll be light enough outside for us to see?"

"Snow always makes things brighter."

"'The moon on the crest of the new-fallen snow,'" she quoted, her eyes dancing.

"Except there's no moon tonight. But that's okay. Wait here while I get my boots, and we'll go to your car together."

Outside the wind had risen, and it howled through the trees, driving the snow every direction, cutting visibility to just a few feet. Now roads were closed all over the Intermountain West.

Amanda watched for Simon out the front window. As soon as he closed the car door, she went out, catching the full force of the wind. Simon hurried toward her and pulled her against the protection of his body.

"Why don't you go back in? I'll handle it." The wind whipped at his words, and he had to lean closer to make her hear.

"I'm okay. You won't know what to bring."

Although at five feet eight, she was not a small woman, Amanda felt small and fragile as he shielded her from the storm. When they reached the car, they found the driver's side was now wedged in snow. Shoveling with their hands, they were able at last to free it. Amanda handed him a large cooler, then pulled out a long, flat box and slammed the door shut. The house lights, shining through the windows, guided them back, welcome and welcoming. The wind didn't seem quite so bad on the return trip, so it didn't take them long to deliver their loads and head back for more.

Maybe it was the short respite, but when they again turned back to the car, Amanda thought the wind was fiercer than ever before. It burned her cheeks, and she pulled her knit cap down until it almost covered her eyes.

"Tell me what to get and go back in. It doesn't make sense for both of us to get cold."

"I'm fine, really," she yelled back. "And once more should be enough. The rest can wait until morning."

When she opened the trunk, Simon stared in amazement. Every corner was crammed with boxes and sacks and packages.

"Did you buy out all of Salt Lake City to make a Christmas for me? I can't believe you would go to this much trouble for a total stranger. Of course, from reading your book, I know what a warm, giving person you are. But this is too much!"

"No. This is the way we always do Christmas!" Only a slight exaggeration. She handed him another cooler. Bigger this time, and heavier. She balanced a large open box on one hip while she slammed the trunk closed, then shifted the box in order to carry it with both hands. In the force of the storm, the lights ahead served as a beacon, and the wind pushed them forward.

Suddenly a gust, stronger than any so far, blasted against them. Helpless to assist him, Amanda watched as Simon fought to keep his balance. She was having difficulty herself and a cry escaped her as she slipped and fell, losing the box and its contents all over the lane.

"Are you okay?" Simon yelled, groping for her through the heavy swirling snow.

"Yes. But I think we just lost the pieces for the gingerbread house." She struggled to her knees and began to search with her hands for the spilled supplies. Simon set down the cooler and helped her.

The search was frustrating. They could hardly see, and every movement was a fight against the wind. Communication was practically impossible. The cold engulfed them.

After finding only two pieces, Amanda turned to Simon and waved her arm toward the house, and he picked up the cooler.

But when she looked toward the house, she could no longer see any lights. Simon cautiously nudged her forward.

"Wait here. I'll see if we're going the right way."

She nodded and he moved forward. After what seemed an eternity, he returned.

"I found it. Come on." Together this time, his arm bracing her back, they challenged the furious wind-driven snow. Stopping only to retrieve the boxes on the edge of the porch, they pushed toward the house. Once inside, Simon put down the cooler and took the box from her hands. Holding the back of her coat, he helped her slip out of it.

"I guess we should have waited until morning. I'm sorry I got you into this," she said, pulling off her cap and shaking her hair loose. With numb fingers, she pushed back the cold, wet strands from her face.

"No, I offered. Are you all right?"

Hanging up her coat, she turned to face him in the dark hall. "Now I am. Are you?"

"Sure. It seems incredible that in one short week I've gone from frying in a jungle to freezing in a blizzard."

"And which is best?"

He laughed. "The best of the worst? I think I'd chose someplace with a median temperature range of twenty degrees. Like

Hawaii."

"Or St. Thomas," Amanda said, trying to keep the longing from her voice.

But Simon shook his head. "No, not St. Thomas. Or anyplace south of the border. In fact, I think I'd choose freezing. But right now, I think we have another problem. No electricity."

Chapter 5

Letter from Spindrift Farm—

> *Nearly every winter we have an ice storm which coats the trees and shrubs, giving our place the look of spun glass, brittle and crystal. We're usually left without electricity for a few hours, or even overnight.*
>
> *All year long I save the remnants of candles—fat and thin, stubby and tall. Whenever the electricity goes off, I put them all on an old brass tray which I place on the coffee table. Their soft flickering light wraps us in coziness.*

Amanda started to laugh.

It wasn't funny. It was disastrous. And yet the laughter kept coming. Her sides began to ache, and she wrapped her arms around her ribs. From the very beginning, one thing after another had gone wrong, and now this. No electricity meant no heat, no hot water, no refrigerator. At least they had a fire, and surely the power would be back on by morning. But would it? After all this was rural Idaho. In the meantime…

"I'm sorry," she gulped. "It's been a long day. Let's go into the living room. At least we have a fire there."

They stood warming their hands over the fire. "By morning we'll be frozen in the bedrooms," she said. "How do you feel about spending the night in front of the fire?"

"You're freezing now."

In fact, she was shaking with the cold. The melting snow ran down her neck and filled her boots, and her wet, icy pants clung to her legs.

"So are you."

Simon grinned. "Then let's get out of these things and put some warm clothes on."

Like three nightgowns, two robes, and several pair of knee socks, she thought as her dislike for the whole experience began to grow. What would happen if she told him the truth? She couldn't predict, so whether she liked it or not, she was stuck in a role that became more untenable with each passing minute. Organizational skills would not make one whit of difference at this point in whether or not she succeeded.

"You'll want to get dry," she said. "There are towels in your bathroom. You should have taken your shower before dinner. I don't know how much hot water there is now."

"There's probably enough for us both to have a quick one, but first we'll need some kind of light. Do you have candles?"

"I don't know."

Simon thought that somehow her sigh sounded more like despair, as if she'd already had too much to cope with and wasn't sure she wanted to handle any more. According to her column, however, today's experiences shouldn't be that unusual during the winter. *What is it about her that doesn't quite fit?* he wondered.

"I'll have to check. We haven't needed them since last winter." Trying to think the way Jenny Canfield would think, based on the precise order of the kitchen, Amanda felt her way through the darkened room to the pantry and searched the three shelves closest to eye level by touch. Finally, near the back but still readily accessible, her fingers found several stocky emergency candles. Beside them, a large box of matches.

"We're in luck, I found them," she called out. When she turned, Simon was standing in the doorway, his arm squared and resting against the frame. Lit from behind by the flickering light from the fireplace, he seemed an intimate part of the house and the night, making her feel safe.

She led the way upstairs and noticed how much darker the hall seemed when he took his candle into the bedroom and shut the door, cutting the amount of light in half.

The water was still hot, and although her shower was quick, the feel of the warmth pelting against her skin was soothing. Amanda felt infinitely better by the time she had finished, dried off, and dressed in the warmest clothes she could find—her long johns and her yellow fleece jogging suit.

Sleeping in front of the fire with Simon Kent was certainly something else she hadn't planned on, and she couldn't quell her nervousness. Whether it was from the whole situation or a reaction to Simon, she didn't know. He seemed almost too good to be true. Ever since she'd broken up with Brett, her social life had been zilch. Salt Lake was a mecca for single women, and it was nearly impossible to find a male over the age of twenty-two who didn't already have a wife or a significant other.

After pulling the covers off the bed and picking up the candle, she realized that trying to carry both at the same time was not only impossible but insane.

Amanda knocked on Simon's door, and he opened it immediately. "I think getting the bedding downstairs is a two-person job."

He followed her back into the master bedroom and picked up the blankets while Amanda held both candles. Then she lit the way down the stairs for him. A second trip stripped the bed in his room.

"Think that will be enough?" she asked.

"With the fire it should be plenty."

The fire burned high, sending shadows dancing around the room, but she studiously ignored the romantic atmosphere.

By spreading the covers from each bed out flat, then folding them in half, they made two beds, each with as much cushion on the bottom as layers on the top. As if by mutual agreement, they placed the two pallets end-to-end, so that they could get equal warmth from the fireplace. It meant sleeping with the top of her head next to the top of his, but that beat sleeping nose to nose.

"Ready for pie?" she asked.

"Let's skip it for tonight unless you want it."

"Rummaging around in a dark kitchen isn't particularly appealing right now," she admitted. Now that she was warm and everything had been taken care of, fatigue pulled at her muscles and made her eyelids heavy. They lay in the flickering darkness, surrounded by the wail of the storm and the crackle of the fire, and occasionally the sounds of their own breathing.

"I used to imagine nights like this," Simon said, breaking the rhythm of the night, his voice both wistful and content.

"Stuck in a snowstorm with no electricity?" she asked wryly.

"There's something cozy and restful about a tight house, and a blazing fireplace when the wind's fierce. When the jungle gets steamy and miserable during the rainy season there's no way to get away from the humidity and the mud. I'll take this any day." In fact, he couldn't have planned a better homecoming than being snowbound, safe, and secure with Laura Reynolds.

Maybe in other circumstances, Amanda thought doubtfully, she would too. But to her, the best alternative would be scuba diving in a clear blue ocean while the sun filled the world with heat and light. She remained silent, however, since this wasn't what Simon would expect from Laura Reynolds.

"You know, I remember storms like this when I was a kid, growing up in Montana. I longed to get snowed in so school would be canceled. Even though the snow was always bad in the winter, we were actually only snowed in a couple of times a year. By afternoon the storm had usually passed, the sun came out, and the world was magic. My brother and I, along with the rest of the kids in town, poured out to go sledding or make snowmen. The streets wouldn't get plowed for nearly a day. My father would be stuck home too, while my mother baked. Later we would make the rounds of all our friends' houses, taking the cookies and brownies."

No wonder he has such a nostalgic bent, growing up like that, Amanda thought. Actually, it sounded like fun.

Impulsively, Amanda said, "My father was in the foreign service. I never lived in a neighborhood where people knew each other from birth. When I look back on it, my life seems like one long adventure, meeting new people, living in new places, experiencing different cultures."

He rolled onto his stomach and propped himself up on his elbows to look at her. Amanda lifted her head to face him. The fire made the gray in his hair look silver and her reflection dance in his eyes. For a moment there was a silent appraisal.

When he'd envisioned spending time with Laura Reynolds, he'd never thought beyond the woman who had wonderful thoughts and ideas about early Americana, a woman who spent her time in the kitchen mixing up one batch of food after another.

Being here, he realized how one-dimensional his thinking had been. Laura was a young, beautiful woman, and despite her graciousness, she didn't seem the type to spend all of her time in the kitchen. The conflicting signals she was sending out made him even more curious.

"I—" A wave of horror swept over Amanda. She caught herself just in time from saying "loved it."

"Hated it." Simon finished for her. "No wonder you're so enthralled with traditional American life."

What a close call! She turned on her back to stare at the ceiling, which was safer than letting him read anything in her face.

"You're right. This place means everything to me. I've loved learning more about the traditions that hold families together and incorporating them into our lives here, and into my writing. No, my life growing up was wonderful, but this is infinitely more precious." That drivel didn't sound like something even Nonnie would write, but this was an emergency. She'd better change the subject, and she'd better not forget again.

"You said you traveled a lot with your job. Where were you before South America?" she asked. There! His life was a safe topic and she could relax.

"Hong Kong. And England before that and New York City before that. It's good to know I'm home permanently now."

"You're serious about not traveling anymore?" How could anyone willingly give that up?

He laughed. "For at least the next twenty years. Then maybe."

"How does an international banker work if he doesn't leave the country?"

"Safely at bank headquarters in San Francisco."

"Well, I predict that in six months you'll be bored to tears stuck in one place," she teased, unable to believe he would ever be content to stay put.

"Boring is being confined to an eight-by-eight hut in a jungle, not living in a large apartment in a city of over a million with dozens of things to do." She could hear the strain in his voice and wished she'd kept quiet. "Whenever I start to long for foreign travel, I'll eat at an ethnic restaurant or go to a foreign film. That will satisfy me. How'd you get interested in writing about life on the farm?"

At least she could be honest about how Laura got started. "I wrote some articles for *Today's Home*, which turned out to be so popular, that the editor asked me to write a monthly column."

"She certainly had a winner there."

"Thanks." Nonnie's column had been one of Amanda's best decisions—coming here, her worst.

Feeling stiff and cramped, Amanda stirred, stretched, turned over and tried to get comfortable. She couldn't. Her bed had never been this uncomfortable before. Her eyes shot open. Where was she?

On the floor!

Spindrift Farm.

Simon Kent.

With a groan, she pulled herself out of the haze of sleep. Every inch of her body seemed to hurt as she shifted again. No wonder camping out in sleeping bags had never appealed to her. At thirty-two, her body was too old to adapt to a hard surface. And worst of all, another day in the wilds! The thought was practically unbearable. She prayed the snow had stopped, and the others were on their way here.

Her eyes drifted around the room, taking in the whitewashed pine tables, the high-backed sofa, and resting on the Priscilla curtains at the window. Now all she could see outside was a blur of white. She squinted. She couldn't seem to distinguish anything else. Oh, no! It was still snowing! Her worst nightmare realized. More snow!

The floor creaked as Simon turned towards the fire. "Good morning, Laura, sleep well?"

"How can you be so cheerful?" Amanda made no effort to disguise her dismay.

Simon laughed. "I'm glad to find out you're not perfect. It's intimidating to be around the world's greatest anything, and particularly to be snowbound with the foremost authority on country living."

If he only knew. The worst of it was, he probably would know soon if the snow kept up much longer and reinforcements didn't arrive. "I hate for you to feel intimidated, so you're free to do anything you see that needs doing." That ought to be some protection from discovery. "But if you'd checked the weather, even you might not be so happy."

"You mean the fact that it's still snowing bothers you?"

"In a word, yes. As long as this keeps up, Paul and the others are still in town while we're here."

"Sorry. I was just enjoying the snow. I forgot that you'd certainly rather have your husband here."

Panic gripped Amanda. She hadn't given the mythical husband a second thought. In fact, on second thought Rob only seemed to add to the peril of being found out. "Of course, I meant Rob. It's just that...uh...since Paul's doing the driving, it's his decision when to come." That sounded lame, but she hoped Simon bought it. "I wonder if the electricity came on during the night?" Amanda hated to move. Even with all her layers of clothing she felt barely comfortable. The fire had died down and getting up in the chilly room didn't appeal to her.

"I need to add a log to the fire, so I'll check." Without any wasted motion, he rose from his bedroll, clicking the light switch to no avail on his way to the porch. "Sorry. We're still without power."

A moment later, Simon returned, his arms loaded with wood, and deftly stoked up the fire. He'd never admit it to Laura, since she seemed upset at the turn of events, but he was looking forward to being snowbound this morning. It made his stay here all the more magic. *I must have missed Christmas traditions more than I thought if I'm romanticizing being snowbound,* he laughed to himself, then said aloud, "The snow is really coming down. I doubt you could see your hand in front of your face out there."

"Dandy!" Amanda had never liked snow. She would have liked to roll up in her blankets, ignoring everything, but she never put off confronting problems. So out she crawled. Facing Simon, she said, "I could stand a solid breakfast." Usually she had a croissant and juice in the morning, but today she was starving. Maybe it was the cold, or the country air, or nerves. "But since Rob was bringing the groceries, there's not much here to fix. How does hot chocolate and apple pie sound?"

"Terrific. I love pie for breakfast."

"You're in luck then. A Monarch range really is a Godsend in a situation like this." She never thought she'd be hearing herself say those words.

"I'll get the fire going."

Amanda gathered up the bedding. "I'll carry my blankets upstairs and splash some water on my face."

Simon grinned at her. "That ought to wake you up for sure. I'll take mine up in a minute, after I get the stove going."

In the bedroom Amanda dumped the bedding unceremoniously on the bed. Br-r, the room was cold, but she couldn't run around all day without brushing her teeth and changing her clothes. Hastily, she splashed icy water over her face and arms, and then she rubbed them briskly with a towel to restore some life. After brushing her chattering teeth, she felt incalculably better. Giving her tangled hair a swipe with her brush, she hurriedly finished in the bathroom.

The air in the bedroom wasn't much warmer than the water, so she quickly shed her clothes and just as quickly, put on some jeans and a red fleece top over a white turtleneck sweater. Except for the jeans, the clothes were soft and cuddly. And cold. Why hadn't she thought about the kitchen? Grabbing a towel and her toiletries, she dashed downstairs.

The kitchen was empty and also degrees warmer than the bedroom as Simon had already started a brisk fire going in the wood range. Depositing her things on the counter, Amanda filled the tea kettle with water, placed it on the stove, and slipped the pie into the oven. Despite the light-hearted exchange last night with Simon, the necessity of maintaining the facade with a myriad of ways she could fail filled her with tension. She'd anticipated it wouldn't be a breeze, but so far, she felt as if she'd done only a marginal job of it. Another twenty-four hours might be twenty-three too many.

When Simon reappeared, his mahogany hair looked damp and slick as if he'd just had a shower. Had the jungle left him brave enough to shower in below freezing temperatures, or was he simply demented from the heat? "Don't tell me you showered!"

"No. I'm not a masochist." He gave her a sardonic look.

"It dawned on me too late that we could save ourselves from chilblains this morning by washing up in here."

"That certainly beats breaking the ice to do it." He took some plates out of the cupboard. "I found a razor in the cabinet that I thought I might use when the water gets hot, if you don't mind. After just getting rid of one beard, I don't feel like starting another."

"Go ahead. However," she teased, "on the practical side, if the weather doesn't clear up, you might be warmer with one."

"I can attest to that. A jungle is a miserable experience with a beard—hot, humid, and itchy." He placed the plates on the table.

Amanda saw that after only twenty minutes in the kitchen last night, he still remembered where everything was. *If he's that observant, I'll need to be doubly on guard,* she warned herself.

"By the way, do you have a transistor radio? Maybe we could get a weather report?"

Her heart dropped. What did she say now? She had no idea if the Canfields had a radio, let alone if it were a transistor. "Uh..." trying to think fast, she said, "I don't know if Rob took it to the city with him or not. Why don't I just call Paul and see how things are there." Going to the wall phone, she picked it up but heard no dial tone. Almost frantically she clicked the receiver, but nothing happened.

She turned to Simon, her frustration showing openly. "Not only don't we have any electricity, the phone is dead." What next? Except she knew what was next. She had to find the radio, which would be like hunting for a needle in a haystack since she couldn't search for it openly. "I'll check upstairs and see if by chance he left it in our bedroom." She hurried out of the room before Simon could say a word.

Once in the bedroom, she couldn't find anything remotely resembling a radio, so she stealthily checked the other upstairs rooms. To her disappointment, none of them had a radio.

She heard Simon's voice calling her. Trying to act casual, she went to the head of the stairs. Simon stood at the bottom, looking up, music coming from a radio that he held in his hands. "I found it. On a bookshelf in the den."

Why didn't I think to check there? she grimaced involuntarily, then asked, "Have they given a weather report?"

"Not yet. Let me try some other stations."

He set the radio on the table, twisted the dial, and looked at Amanda with a smile as a voice said, "Good morning, folks. In case you've just joined us, the weather bureau is forecasting at least forty-eight more hours of snow. A stalled low pressure has dumped over twenty inches of snow on us already, and there is no indication when it might move on. The wind is gusting up to hurricane force, and the state police have reported that all roads out of Salt Lake City and into the surrounding states are closed. People are requested to stay indoors, unless it is a life or death emergency."

Oh, no! What had she ever done to deserve this? She'd always tried to live right. She'd been good to widows and orphans! She'd even taught the Beehives! What had she done to be quarantined with Simon Kent in the middle of nowhere?

Amanda stared at Simon in horror as the radio voice droned on. "And if that isn't enough for you folks, a transformer supplying electricity to Wyoming, Utah, and Idaho blew out during the night causing a widespread power outage. Power company officials tell us that although they have all crews working on it, they don't know when they'll have it repaired."

How on earth could she keep up this pretense for forty-eight hours? Just a few minutes ago she'd been worried about twenty-four more hours. Now her sentence had been doubled. That was just great. She could kiss her entire career good-bye, thanks to one bright idea and a badly timed snowstorm.

Trying not to let her real feelings show, Amanda forced a smile. "Is this old-fashioned enough for you?" she asked Simon pleasantly.

"Actually, I'm looking forward to it. We have plenty of wood and food. It reminds me of—"

"Your childhood?" she asked in amazement.

"No, your column," he grinned.

Amanda thought of Nonnie's words. The entire staff had loved that particular column, and Amanda had thought her subscribers would be equally enthusiastic. Now she decided that Nonnie and her fans were completely insane. How had she ever imagined this would work?

Simon gave her a reassuring smile, but now it only made her edgier. "Just don't expect brownies from me," she warned, "I'm not your mother."

"You're right there. You're not even remotely like her!" His expression said that, even with disheveled hair and a pale face, Laura Reynolds was like no mother he'd ever known. "But I'd still like to try your brownies."

"Sorry. This morning you'll have to settle for pie and hot chocolate." She brought the gallon-sized can of cocoa mix from the pantry and placed it on the counter.

Simon fiddled with the radio until he found an easy-listening station that filled the kitchen with the warm strains of Mantovani. "How's that? Take your mind off the storm?"

"It's better than the news."

Amanda put cocoa in the cups and Simon added the hot water. As he stirred the mix, she removed the pie from the warming oven and dished it up.

Amanda smiled at the bliss on his face as he savored the first bite.

"You know, Laura, my mother and grandmother made wonderful pastry, but I've got to hand it to you. You make the flakiest crust I've ever eaten."

"Thank you." Amanda had to agree. If she had to take credit for making it, she couldn't ask for something better than this. She doubted that even Nonnie could do any better.

Pushing his plate aside, Simon leaned forward and rested his chin on his hand and looked at her intently. Amanda felt uncomfortable, if she looked that bad maybe she'd brave the ice water and take a shower. Before she could say anything, he laughed. "Maybe it's because of the way you're wearing your hair, but you don't look like the photo on the back of your book. And I'm having a hard time picturing you in this house. You seem more like a city girl, more at home in Salt Lake City than on a farm." His face crinkled with amusement.

"Are you sure you're not just pretending that you live here?" he teased.

Amanda felt herself tense up. "I love being here. There is a peacefulness in the country that you just don't find elsewhere. I could never live in the city without knowing that I had a retreat in the country." Peaceful? Maybe if anything had been even marginally under control, she would have found the country peaceful.

Simon stretched in satisfaction. "I'll stack the dishes, chief, while you plan our day." He carried their dishes to the sink, then picked up the sponge and wiped the table and the counter.

Plan their day? What did she have to work with? The ingredients were still in Salt Lake, the decorations were a small blizzard away in her car, and the power was off. A day like this took plenty of planning all right. How could they possibly get through the next forty-eight hours with nothing to do?

She looked at the supplies they'd rescued last night. It would be much easier if everything she'd brought were stashed away in cupboards, as if it had been there forever, instead of coming out of the trunk of her car like an afterthought. Well, he'd accepted that she and Rob had been away for several weeks, and maybe that in itself would explain it.

"Since the power's out, I guess we could put the things we brought in on the back porch."

"Sure."

When they'd finished, Simon sat back down and picked up his cocoa. "Got any cards?"

Did that man know how to say anything that didn't put her on the spot? Simon Kent undoubtedly thought he was being the undemanding house guest. Instead he was making her a nervous wreck.

"I'm not much of a card player," she answered, "so I don't know if Rob has any or not. Why don't you check in the den?" That seemed like a likely place since he'd found the radio there.

As soon as he left the room, she yanked open the drawers in the kitchen. Nothing. She hurried to the dining room and checked the breakfront. Crystal and tablecloths. Finally on the top shelf in the hall closet she found some board games. Zion, BYopoly, and Scrabble. Relief! Here was something they could do if Simon couldn't find any cards, and best of all, she could walk right to the closet and get them. Of course, she was a cinch to win since he obviously wasn't Mormon.

She could survive the next few days, but she was certain to age years in doing so. The next time she used the bathroom she would check in the mirror for gray hair.

As Simon came out of the den, Amanda hastily slammed the closet door shut, almost leaping out of the hall into the living room. She could feel her heart tripping like a jackhammer as she breathed to herself, *The last thing I need is for him to see that I was looking for the cards, too!*

"Success. You were right. Rob keeps his cards in there." Simon waved the deck of cards in his hand. "Ready to get beaten?"

She took a deep, calming breath. "I wouldn't get too cocky if I were you." How long could she keep him entertained playing cards? All day? Half the night?

"Played much?"

She didn't like the gleam in his eye. "A little," she said tentatively, not wanting to give herself away. "A long time ago. In my wild misspent youth." She didn't intend to divulge to Simon all the times she'd sneaked out and played cards with members of the embassy staff when they were posted to remote places.

Amanda made more hot chocolate while Simon shuffled and dealt.

"Now which ones are spades?" she asked in mock naiveté, although she really did have a hard time telling spades and clubs apart.

Simon's brows raised, and he gave her a penetrating look. "The ones that resemble little shovels." She could tell from his expression that he thought she was a pushover.

Her eyes narrowed thoughtfully. "Why don't we play for stakes?"

"A penny a point?" He gave her a condescending smile.

"How about the loser fixes lunch?" With her experience, she was sure she could beat him, and that way she could get out of doing the cooking on that miserable stove.

"Agreed. Let's play until noon. Whoever's ahead wins."

Amanda hid a smile and told herself comfortably, *Like taking candy from a baby*. For the first time since she met Simon, she felt on safe ground.

Attempting to lull him into carelessness, she made no effort to win the first hand. He grinned arrogantly, although he had a twinkle in his eye when he beat her again on the second hand. The minute he dealt her last card on the third hand, she decided to go for it. What a hand! Only one card that didn't fit. She'd easily find another one that would work and discard it. Finally she did, but not before Simon had laid down a number of cards. She won the hand by twenty points, although she was still far behind Simon's total points for the game.

"You're not such a bad player," Simon said. "That was a good game."

Good game? She had played better when she was ten. She groaned inwardly when she looked at her new hand.

Again she won but only by ten points. Darn! Not enough to equal his score.

"Way to go," Simon said easily. Amanda thought his tone was condescending.

"Patronizing me?" she challenged him, but he only grinned.

Enough is enough! she said silently, glaring at him. *I'm going to clean you out this time.*

She dealt the cards, and miracle of miracles, she got three aces. Should she lay them down? No, she'd go out all at once. Surprise him. But she was starting to feel desperate until she finally picked up the fourth ace. She sighed a breath of relief. Simon's hand evidently wasn't too good because he hadn't put down anything, and he picked up the pile. Good she'd be able to go out and leave him with a fistful of counters.

He surprised her. "Gin!" he said. She looked in horror as he lay down his entire hand.

"A hundred and thirty points plus twenty," Simon all but crowed.

"How did you do that?" she demanded. "Cheat?"

"Laura Reynolds accusing a guest of cheating?" he said, his eyes gleaming with amusement. "Isn't that against Amy Vanderbilt's rules of etiquette?"

"You've got that mixed up with the rules of the old West. Amy Vanderbilt says in her section on Etiquette for the Snowbound that the first thing you do is establish that no one is cheating," she said firmly. "Now, did you cheat?"

Simon looked thoughtful. "Did she mention what kind of cheating? This could be interesting."

"Cards."

At the look on her face, Simon chuckled. "Laura, playing cards with you is like taking candy from a baby."

Her words exactly! Good grief, they even thought alike!

He nodded toward her cards. "How many points in your hand?"

She slapped them down on the table. "See for yourself. Seventy!" She sank back in her seat and closed her eyes. Was there any way to get out of doing the cooking?

Chapter 6

Letter from Spindrift Farm—

Time passes all too quickly when we're entertaining friends. In the hustle and bustle of our lives, it seems we never have enough time to just sit and visit, catch up on all the happenings in their lives. Probably the greatest gift we could give others, besides gifts of the heart, would be time. Time with no pressing duties. Time to explore our hopes and dreams.

"I have a feeling I'll be fixing lunch," Amanda said in mock humility. Nevertheless she intended to trounce him thoroughly.

A self-satisfied smile curled Simon's lips. "Exactly what I had in mind. You didn't really expect to win, did you?"

"Is that so impossible? I've won two hands already." However, at the rate she was going they might be the last two.

"Well, considering the fact that I let you win," he drawled, cutting them each another piece of pie, "yes, it is. I let you win because you looked so down in the mouth after the first two hands. I just wanted to cheer you up."

"You wanted to cheer me up?" She stared at him in disbelief. *So much for lulling him*, she thought in disgust.

"Certainly," Simon smiled. "But not, of course, lose a meal cooked by Laura Reynolds." His smile revealed two dimples, but she refused to be sidetracked by them.

"This is war," she announced as she slapped the cards down on the table to deal the next hand.

Not wanting to get caught with a handful, she laid down the cards she could. With her next turn, she tossed back her long blond hair triumphantly and practically shouted "Gin."

They continued playing, the score seesawing back and forth. Amanda glanced at her watch. "Just time for one more hand before lunch." She didn't really feel like eating after all the pie and cocoa they'd had, but she was 120 points ahead.

Then she lost the last hand. When the final score was totaled, she had lost the game by five points. Five little points meant she was stuck with the cooking.

"Well, Laura, what's for lunch?" Simon picked up the cards and shuffled them before placing them in the box. Standing, he stretched. "I'll check on the fires while you fix the food."

"You mean you're actually hungry?" she asked incredulously.

"What else is there to do?" he said, lifting the plate on the stove and stirring the fire.

"You've got a point there," she said. "I've had enough of cards."

Simon went out on the back porch and brought in an armload of wood, dropping it on the floor next to the stove. With some careful maneuvering he placed one of the larger pieces inside.

Just then a cheerful voice broke into the music on the radio said, "Here's the latest on the storm that has buried the Mountain West today. Weather forecasters are still predicting forty-eight hours more of snow, and they see no end in sight."

"Have you ever noticed how often the weathermen are wrong? Why now of all times do they seem to be right on target!" Amanda said, turning the volume up on the radio.

"Easy. They can just look out their windows and predict. It hardly takes instruments or technical knowledge to tell we're buried in snow."

"Well, if they'd been a little more accurate yesterday, we'd both be in Salt Lake instead of stranded here." Her eyes darkened at the thought.

"I think I prefer here." His lips curved into a half smile that seemed to hint, "and you're the reason."

What could she say? *I still prefer the city and you're the reason.* No, she couldn't let him know that she was only Laura Reynold's inept granddaughter. She gave him a weak smile. "I guess it could be worse." She turned at the sound of the radio.

"...still hopes to restore electricity today, but with the storm the work is progressing slowly. Some localized areas in Idaho are experiencing disruption of their phone service. We have no more information, but we'll keep you updated on any changes as we get them. Now here's a song to lighten the news..." Once again the strains of violin music invaded the kitchen.

"Back to the really important news—what's for lunch?" Simon said, putting a pan of water on the stove.

"Has anyone ever told you that you have a one-track mind?"

"Yes. Only they weren't referring to food."

"Somehow that surprises me," Amanda retorted, stretching out her long legs under the table, and making no move to get up. "I would have thought being a good cook was the first prerequisite on your list of potential candidates for 'wifedom.'"

He cocked his eyebrow. "It is now. Before, 'wifedom,' as you so quaintly put it, wasn't on my agenda. Now back to the important stuff. What's for lunch?"

"Okay. Okay. I'll check the freezer." Amanda doubted that Jenny would have any "fast foods" cached away. She found chicken in the freezer but no other kind of meat. After selecting what looked like a cherry pie, another loaf of bread, and a package of chicken, she found some of Grandma's Frozen Homemade Egg Noodles. It made her smile to realize that Jenny also used prepared foods. Pulling off the label, she stuffed it in her pocket. Let Simon think that these were Laura's Homemade Egg Noodles. In much better spirits, she returned to the kitchen.

"How does chicken noodle soup with homemade noodles sound? It'll take at least an hour, so if you don't think you can last that long, there's still some pie left."

"You're a lifesaver!" He slid the last piece of pie onto his plate. "Do you raise your own chickens? I admire your self-sufficiency."

Amanda looked at the chicken she was rinsing. The freezer wrap didn't look commercial so they probably did. "Uh...yes."

"Do you like picking chickens and then cleaning them? I helped my grandmother once, and once was enough for me." He grimaced at the memory. "The feathers stuck to my fingers, and I thought I'd never get them off."

Since she'd never had the experience, Amanda didn't know what to say. Why did he have to be so curious about farm life? The fact that Laura Reynolds lived here ought to be enough. Did he have to be interested in all the little details of her life that could so easily trip Amanda up? What did she say now? "Rob does it," she shrugged.

Her answer puzzled Simon. She had a strange diffidence about her life on the farm, and yet at the same time, she seemed to cook almost effortlessly. He wondered why she seemed to hem and haw every time the conversation rolled around to her life on the farm.

Amanda hummed as she popped the chicken into a pot and covered it with water, adding seasonings from Jennie's spice shelf. Then she turned to Simon.

"Now how about another game of gin rummy?"

Simon was amused. "You're kidding! You want to get beaten again."

Amanda flashed him a conspiratorial grin. "I don't intend to lose."

"Let me give you some advice. Stick to something you know—like cooking," Simon said loftily. She made a face at him and Simon felt his heart thump slowly. He found her fallibility at cards and her determination to win captivating, especially in light of her obvious competence in the kitchen.

"Okay," she said easily. "Since you won't let me beat you at cards, excuse me while I find something to read." As she passed

Simon, he caught the scent of her perfume and involuntarily moved toward her before he caught himself. *Watch it*, he warned himself. *She already has a husband.*

Amanda stared out the window. Four hours down. Only forty-four more to go before the snow was projected to stop. What if the weathermen were wrong and it lasted even longer? A thought too horrible even to contemplate. How could she keep him entertained?

If only she'd met Simon somewhere else and under different circumstances. Amanda could think of a thousand things she'd enjoy doing with an attractive man. Finding an eligible male in Salt Lake was nearly impossible, and now here she was snow-bound with someone who seemed almost too good to be true. Single, witty, a good sense of humor. And wouldn't you know, she was stuck playing the role of a happily married woman. A deep, heartfelt sigh escaped her lips.

Simon certainly wasn't like Brett. She hadn't thought of Brett for ages—why now? Probably because anytime she'd had two thoughts about a man, the specter of her ex-fiancé haunted her. A major mistake in her love life that was enough to last a lifetime.

When she'd first moved to Salt Lake, she had met Brett at her grandfather's law office. He'd seemed the epitome of what she wanted: a returned missionary, bright, ambitious, a lawyer who was going places in the firm. But she soon found he also had an ultra-conservative attitude with rigid ideas about how women should dress and act. At first she had considered herself lucky and set out to make herself over, so she would be exactly what he wanted.

She understood that he absolutely did not want her to have a career and that he wanted her to devote her energies to raising their kids, entertaining friends and guests, and promoting his career. She understood that she would be forever an appendage, never to step out of her husband's shadow.

The last straw had been her hair, of all the dumb things. She'd had it frizzed without getting his approval. Brett told her he thought she looked ridiculous.

"I don't care," she had responded. "It doesn't matter. I'm really not interested anymore in your approval." And she realized that it was true. Even now she laughed to herself at the memory of the look on his face. Brett had been completely stunned. It was the first time she'd ever seen someone blanch.

"Furthermore," she went on, "I prefer a career, and I don't plan on ever marrying." That wasn't one hundred percent accurate—she actually wanted to marry and was even willing to put her family first. But she would not to be ordered to do it.

Besides, what woman wants a husband who doesn't want her the way she is? Amanda liked herself and she didn't ever plan on being someone else—although these last few days she'd felt like a few changes might not be such a bad idea.

Which brought her back to the immediate problem—how to keep Simon occupied. Jenny undoubtedly had sugar and corn syrup, so possibly they could make some candy canes. But Amanda found it hard to marshall up any enthusiasm. The candy might not turn out, and she dreaded another failure in front of Simon. On the other hand, the candy canes might turn out perfectly, in which case she would be missing an opportunity for the photographer to record the momentous event. Amanda sighed. No matter what she did, it might be wrong.

Wandering into the living room, wondering what to do with herself, she plumped up the sofa pillows and stretched out on the couch in front of the fire. It had burned almost completely to charcoal, the flame just nipping at the unburned ends of logs. If she had noticed that no heat reached the couch before she lay down, she would have thrown on more wood. As it was, she felt too tired to move.

"No wonder you forced that pie on me. You were after the couch," Simon accused, standing at the door looking down at her.

"No one has to be forced to eat Laura Reynolds's pies," she

retorted and threw a pillow at him.

He neatly dodged and caught the pillow with one hand. Before she realized his intentions, it landed on her face.

She watched as Simon hunkered down by the fire, the muscles rippling the dark tan of his arms. To make room for more firewood, he began moving what was left of the logs with the poker. Amanda was startled for a moment as the full force of Simon's masculine appearance struck her. He really fit in here on the farm, more than she ever would.

"You're so handy at roughing it. How did you ever end up in a bank? I would have thought you would have been a farmer or a rancher."

He grinned. "My family's always been in banking."

She was astonished. "What were all those homespun stories you were telling me last night? Just that—stories?"

"No. My grandfather owned a bank in a small town outside of Butte, Montana, but he lived on a farm. Later the bank was absorbed into a large statewide system. My grandfather retired, and my father became vice-president of the banking organization."

"So how come you didn't stay in Montana?"

"My brother and I both went east to school, and neither one of us moved back. I found large cities more exciting than small towns."

Amanda gave him a calculating look, then couldn't resist saying, "I think you'd have an easier time finding a wife who wears an apron if you were a farmer. Women who marry international bankers expect parties, glamour, travel"—she waved her hand in the air to emphasize each word. "They don't plan on staying home every night laboring over a hot stove."

"Boy, are you jumping to conclusions. In this day and age, most farm wives have to work in town just to stay on the farm. And although international bankers travel, their wives usually stay home."

"How disillusioning! A word of advice, Simon. Don't explain

yourself to any hapless woman you might be interested in, or she'll never have you." Her green eyes twinkled with merriment.

"How do you advise me to win her then?"

"I'd rely on the Simon Kent charm and flash her your little boy smile. She'll be so dazzled, she won't question anything."

Amanda smiled at him from over the top of the pillow she cradled against her chest.

"Is that how Rob won you?"

"Never! I pride myself on being able to see beyond charm and white teeth."

"Ouch! That hurts."

"Present company excluded."

"Now tell me, where did you study Home Ec? For some reason, I have a hard time seeing you as a Home Ec major."

Amanda shook her finger at him. "Now you're jumping to conclusions. I chose UCLA for the sun and the surf. Along the way I got a degree in creative writing. Afterwards I attended Stanford's publishing workshop."

No wonder she didn't seem the type, Simon thought. She wasn't. "How did you end up in Salt Lake? You seem like the quintessential California Golden Girl."

"Actually I thought New York City was where it was at, and so I moved there. My first job was as an editorial assistant with a large publishing house. Since there were dozens of us huddled around the bottom rung of the ladder, I quickly figured out I wouldn't have a meteoric rise to the top. In between reading the manuscript of every first novel written in the United States, I wrote some freelance articles, hoping the experience might get me a job on a magazine. And it did."

"Just like that?" Simon snapped his fingers.

She laughed. "If you're a slow snapper. Actually it was nearly three years and across the country to Utah. Until then I never did make enough to quit the publishing house."

"What about Rob?" She hadn't mentioned him once, and yet from everything he'd read, Rob was involved totally in her life.

Now she looked puzzled.

"What about him?"

"Why didn't your husband support you while you got started?"

She looked startled. "The chicken!" She jumped up and darted into the kitchen, calling behind her, "I've got to add the noodles!"

Simon realized she hadn't answered his question. *What is it that's wrong?* he wondered.

"How long did you say you'd been at Spindrift Farm?" Simon tried again later.

"Five years." That was as long as Laura had been writing her column and Amanda had been editor.

Simon watched her carefully, trying to read what she wasn't telling him. She seemed surprisingly reluctant to talk about her husband. Were they having problems?

Before he could ask her anything else, Amanda looked at her watch deliberately. "I think it's time to eat."

What is she hiding? Simon asked himself.

Amanda devised a plan to avoid continuing their conversation. After lunch she led him to the dining room and shook the Scrabble box invitingly.

Simon accepted the challenge. "Now we'll see how much education you managed to squeeze in with all that sun and surf."

They each chose a Scrabble piece to see who would begin. Amanda chose L. Simon revealed his W. He picked up seven tiles and studied them intently.

"O-t-t-e-r. Thirty-six points. Not bad for the first word."

Amanda leaned across the coffee table and made o-x-f-o-r-d-s. "Plain serviceable shoes your downtrodden wife will be wearing. Twenty-four points." Lunch had gone smoothly and she hoped she could keep him occupied with Scrabble the rest of the day.

"R-o-p-e. Watch your tongue or you might be hung. Double word. Twenty-eight points." He quickly jotted down his score.

Amanda frowned at her letters, trying to figure out a word using q. A fierce gust of wind shook the house, rattling the windows again. For an instant she thought the large one in the living room would break.

"Can't make a word this time?" Simon gloated.

"Dream on!" Giving up on the q, she lay down s-t-v-e across the o. "What your poor wife will be slaving over. Fourteen points." She smiled triumphantly. "We writers have superior vocabularies."

"So do we bankers."

Amanda looked on in astonishment as Simon filled in the squares between a bunch of unrelated letters and made v-o-c-a-b-u-l-a-r-i-e-s. "No one can do that!"

"I just did." He began counting his points. "With double letters and double word points I have—let's see—eighty-nine points."

Amanda groaned. "I can't stand people who crow when they win." Despite her words, though, she enjoyed the cozy, intimate feeling as she reached over for a sofa cushion to sit on. The rage of the storm outside and the warmth of the burning logs inside enveloped them in an rosy glow of camaraderie she hadn't felt since her friendships with the various embassy staffs. A snowbound Christmas was a far cry from St. Thomas, but as she lay sprawled on the floor surrounded by Scrabble tiles, she could almost forget that the attractive man across from her thought she was a completely different person from who she really was.

"Have you gone to sleep? I'm thirteen points ahead."

His words brought her back to reality. "Only until I have my turn, but it's almost too dark to see what we're doing. I think we need the candles." She cautiously felt her way through the dining room and into the kitchen for matches.

Grateful for the firelight as she re-entered the dining room, she told Simon, "We only have two candles left and they're getting pretty small. Maybe we better just burn one at a time so they'll last." She lit one and placed it on the coffee table next to the game board. Then she resumed her position on the floor. "Abe Lincoln might have enjoyed reading by firelight, but I need something a little brighter."

"I don't think Scrabble counts as serious reading." He pulled his knee up to his chest and rested his forearm on it. Her breath caught at the intimate gleam in his eyes, and she turned quickly away. "Don't you have kerosene lamps?"

Amanda's heart sank. Surely if Ben and Jenny had one they'd keep it in the living room. She glanced around the room; none were visible, and she didn't remember any in the kitchen. No time for a quick, unobtrusive search of the house, Amanda thought wryly. And she could hardly say that Rob might have taken them to Salt Lake. After an awkward moment of silence, she said simply, "No."

Simon was surprised. "I would've thought that kerosene lamps would be a necessity here. Do the lights go out often?"

How would she know? "Not that often."

They continued the game, but Amanda felt jumpy. A feeling of impending doom clouded her mind and the only words she could think of were *it, was* and *an*. Hardly winners. Finally, she said, "Let's put the game away for awhile. We'd better concentrate on supper before the candles burn out and it's too dark to see in the kitchen."

Scrambling to his feet, Simon picked up one of the candles. "Good idea. I'll use this one to go upstairs for a minute."

Amanda leaned back against the couch, her legs in front of her and stared at the fire. The hypnotic flickering of the flames held her captive until she heard Simon come down the stairs. As she turned towards him, she felt the blood drain from her face. For the life of her she couldn't think of a single word of explanation as he stood there with a kerosene lamp in each hand. Each lamp was completely full. She gripped the coffee table, clutching it as if it were a lifeline.

Simon spoke deliberately. "I thought you said you didn't have a kerosene lamp. There was one in the bathroom and the bed-room." He stared intently at Amanda, waiting for her to say something.

"I…uh…" What could she say? How could she not know what was in her own house? Her mind was blank. How could she possibly extricate herself from this mess? As she groped for something or someone, Rob came to mind. Good old Rob. Although her muscles seemed frozen, she attempted to smile brightly. Her heart pounded so hard she could barely get the words past her lips. "Rob must have bought them. We'd discussed it, but I hadn't realized he'd gotten them already."

Simon was silent as he set one of the lamps on the table and lit it. Amanda scarcely dared to look at him. Would he believe her? What if he didn't?

What would he say if she told him the truth? Amanda considered the possibility, but shook her head. She couldn't risk it. For all his kindness and despite the comfort she felt with him, Simon was still a stranger she'd met less than twenty-four hours ago. If he chose, he could jeopardize the reputation of the magazine.

Her heart pounded painfully in her chest and the fear nauseated her. Why would anyone ever want to lie? Just trying to keep track of all the details was murder. More than ever, she doubted she'd be able to pull this off.

Simon spoke at last. "Well, no matter how you got them, we're in luck. I don't know why I hadn't noticed the lamps before. But no more reading by firelight."

After supper, they continued playing Scrabble until Amanda conceded defeat. No one could win who could only think of two and three-letter words. Although the kerosene lamp issue had been resolved, Amanda was still shaken from the close call. She found it impossible to think clearly. Simon couldn't help but be suspicious when she stuttered and then came up with such inane answers. She didn't know how much longer she could pretend to be the competent manager of Spindrift Farm.

Simon yawned and then stretched. "Time for bed. What do you think?"

"You're right. After this scintillating, fun-filled day, I'm ready for sleep."

Simon offered to carry the bedding down. "You're assigned to light the way."

"Sounds fair." There was no incentive to linger upstairs with the freezing temperature. So after a quick trip to the bathroom, she grabbed the jogging suit she'd worn the night before and met Simon in the hall. "I speak for the kitchen first," she said as she led the way downstairs.

"Don't guests go first?"

"Ladies before gentlemen!"

He laughed and dropped the bedding on the couch before returning upstairs and Amanda dashed to the kitchen.

Amanda fixed their beds the same way as the night before. It had seemed to work well. Wrapping the blankets snugly around her, she propped herself up on one elbow and watched while Simon banked the fire. Then she lay flat on her back and listened to the sound of the wind pelting the snow against the windows. Every once in a while the house would creak as a particularly violent gust hit it. This storm could be her undoing. The more she and Simon were together in these intimate surroundings, the harder it became to resist his easy-going charm. And she had to. In order to survive she had to. Somehow she had to remain warm but distant. Easy enough to say, but practically impossible to do.

"Asleep?" Simon asked, slipping into his bedroll.

Amanda didn't answer. Now wasn't the time for a heart-to-heart.

Chapter 7

Letter from Spindrift Farm—

> *We're content to stay home during the cold months. We spend our time reading seed and bulb catalogs, planning for our summer gardens.*

Amanda crawled out of her makeshift bed and looked out the window. Still snowing! The snow was up to the window sill, and if it hadn't been for the wind, the drift probably would have been higher. Another land-mined day to look forward to. By now Simon had questioned her about every possible detail of living in this house. Surely he couldn't find any more questions to trip her. Like kerosene lamps.

She sighed. If only it would stop snowing. She felt so defenseless. Defenseless? Ridiculous. She'd never felt defenseless in her life. She hardly recognized herself. *Be friendly, but reserved*, she ordered herself sternly.

"How'd you sleep?"

Startled to hear Simon's voice, Amanda turned towards the makeshift beds. He was poking at the logs in the fireplace.

"Fine." Once she'd finally fallen asleep, she'd slept soundly. But the worries that had kept her awake still troubled her this morning.

Moving away from the window, she said, "Let's check the

radio. See if hope is in sight. I've never heard of a storm lasting this long. Surely the weather forecasters are wrong."

She listened glumly to the update. "...the parts are at Los Angeles International Airport just waiting to be shipped when there's a break in the weather here. Until then no power. Thirty-six inches of snow have fallen since the storm commenced Friday afternoon, and they are predicting at least fifty before the storm moves out..."

"Fifty inches of snow!" She quickly calculated. "Four feet two inches! Have you ever heard of that much before?"

"Only at ski resorts. This should make skiing good next week at Park City."

"If the wind keeps blowing, this place will be like living in an igloo."

"But only for a couple of days. Surely by then we'll be rescued by your husband and the intrepid photographer."

"Oh, sure." She tried not to be sarcastic, but somehow she didn't have much faith in them adding anything but problems to an already ticklish situation.

Picking up her bedding, Amanda started upstairs, with Simon following closely behind her. The bedroom was even colder than it had been before, if that were possible. The downstairs seemed familiar and homey, the bedroom and bath like foreign territory. Amanda didn't want to stay here a moment longer than necessary. She grabbed her jeans and sweaters and ran downstairs, where she draped her clothes across a chair to warm next to the stove. To her delight when she slipped them on, they were warm.

Then she ran back upstairs to the bathroom. Too bad there wasn't a mirror in the kitchen. On the other hand, she thought when she glimpsed herself in the dim light of the bathroom, it was a good thing she wasn't constantly reminded that her hair was looking more scraggly than crimped. Not wanting to look totally wiped out, she carefully put on make-up.

Simon was adding wood to the stove when she entered the kitchen again. He put the cover on the range, and Amanda could see the approval in his eyes when he said, "You're looking perky!"

"You look kind of perky yourself." It amazed her that anyone could keep this man captive for six months. One smile from him and any normal person would have released him on the spot. Of course, those people weren't normal, and they weren't women.

After breakfast, after the dishes, Simon turned to her with serious intent in his eyes. "When are you starting your Christmas cooking? My mouth watered as I read all those delicious-sounding recipes in your column. That's one of the reasons I accepted your invitation."

"We won't have most of the ingredients that we need until Rob and Becki get here," Amanda answered, feigning a hint of regret. Not that they would be any help cooking on a wood stove. But they had to do something. "Maybe we could make candy canes? If we have any corn syrup left."

In the pantry, she located both sugar and syrup. She wasn't wildly enthusiastic, but what could go wrong? She had the recipe, she could read, and she'd seen Nonnie do it. Surely she could do it too.

"Let me get the recipe. I think it's with the things on the back porch." She found it along with the slushy fruit puree used for flavoring.

"I'm surprised you don't have it memorized," Simon commented without any expression in his voice.

Amanda found a ready lie. "Too many recipes in my head. I get all the ingredients confused."

But he had another question. "Do you have molds?"

This time she had no quick answer. "Molds?" she asked blankly. Then it came to her. "This is a taffy recipe, so we have to pull the canes into shape. No molds." She wiggled her fingers at him, then looked pointedly at his hands. That was a mistake. His hands weren't designed for candy making, they were made for caressing and, knowing him, even tickling. Amanda would have been the first to volunteer as the subject, but she hurriedly forced the image aside. "And you've kept your fingers in fantastic shape with your double dealing," she teased.

Simon looked offended. "Now, Laura, don't confuse an expert player with a cardsharp!"

"Whatever gave you that idea?" she said innocently. "A guilty conscience!"

His raised eyebrows gave him a rakish look. "Is there a rule I don't know about, such as 'Don't ever beat your hostess at cards'?"

"Only if you want to be invited back!"

Amanda waved him back from the stove, propped the recipe card against a canister, and started measuring sugar. She adroitly managed to keep the right things happening in the right order. But that wasn't quite good enough. The recipe was never intended for a wood range.

At first the fire wasn't hot enough, but when Simon stirred up the embers, the mixture boiled almost immediately. Afraid that the candy would overcook, Amanda practically snatched it off the stove only to wind up with a sticky mess.

"Am I expected to pull that?" Simon asked, looking appalled. "I think you've discovered a new formula for handcuffs. Once we got it on our hands, we'd never get free." He picked up a wooden paddle and tried stirring the candy, but the handle just stuck upright in the goo. The candy seemed as determined to hold onto the paddle as Simon was to get it out. With one final yank, it came free, sending him reeling back a few steps.

He gave her a sly grin. "When I consented to spend the week with you, no one informed me I would be held prisoner by a batch of candy."

"Relax. It's water soluble," Amanda said dryly, thankful the photographer wasn't here shooting pictures of her failure.

"It's hard to believe you're an expert at making this," Simon said matter-of-factly.

Obviously, she wasn't, but she decided to shift the blame. "Temperatures are so critical when you're making something like this." That and practical experience. She'd watched Nonnie make it a hundred times, and she'd pulled the finished product into canes. What did Nonnie do that she wasn't doing?

She was aware that Simon didn't comment that while temperatures were critical to cooking taffy, she had no doubt made it hundreds of times on this stove, hadn't she?

As he stood there silently, Amanda tried to speak briskly, "Why don't you toss that mess out. Maybe the birds would like it. Then re-butter the platter while I measure the ingredients for some more." She picked up the measuring cup once again.

"The birds will have to wait," Simon said, coming back into the kitchen. "That stuff sank like lead, and I'm sure it won't be found until the spring thaw."

"Good. I like to bury my mistakes."

Although the thermometer registered hard ball, Amanda let the taffy cook an extra few minutes. She didn't trust the thermometer and she didn't want any more sticky goo on her hands. To her horror, the candy thermometer quickly shot up too high, and she couldn't even break the crystal mass. Without a word, Simon carried it out the back door.

Amanda was tempted to give up, but Laura Reynolds's reputation was at stake. She reached for the sugar again. Almost gone. One way or another this would be the last batch.

"The third time's the charm," she said lightly, although she didn't believe that for a minute. This candy was doomed to failure.

It must have been charmed because the canes turned out. Oh, not perfectly. The shapes had a definite uneven homemade look that Nonnie's hadn't, but they were recognizable, and that's all she could ask for at this point. She only wished Paul had been there to get pictures of them pulling the taffy and twisting the different strands into fat delicious-looking canes. The amazing thing was she'd pulled it off—somehow Simon continued to respect her kitchen acumen.

Another morning down, thank goodness, but an afternoon and evening to go. Never before had Amanda watched the hours pass so slowly.

"What do you want for lunch?" She slid into the chair across the table from Simon. "Have you noticed there's nothing to think of here, but food?" And making it through this ordeal.

"Laura Reynolds, you surprise me! I thought that was your main interest in life!"

The challenge in his blue eyes unnerved her, and she said flippantly, "How boring! And especially when we're limited to chicken. Unfortunately, I don't have my 101 Ways to Cook Chicken with me." She stood up and went out to the freezer for another package. Unwrapping the chicken, she placed it in the sink to thaw.

"Tell me, if Laura Reynolds doesn't like to think about food all the time, what does she think about?"

"Museums, musicals, mysteries, basketball—"

"Basketball?" The surprise in his voice was obvious.

"Yes, basketball. I never miss a Jazz home game."

"You don't?" He sounded shocked. "You're really a fan if you make a five-hour drive each way, two or three times a week, just to see them play. That's devotion."

Good grief! Who in their right mind would drive from here into Salt Lake City in the winter to see all the home games? And she'd just announced in no uncertain terms that she did! She messed with the faucet trying to hide her discomfort. "Uh...I try to schedule my business meetings on game days."

"That sounds logical." But Simon wondered at her the nervous stutter. It couldn't still be him, could it? It was hard to believe that she was so uncomfortable around him. In fact, he felt such a kinship with her, he had a hard time remembering he hadn't always known her. "Who got you interested? Rob?"

"No, he didn't," she said shortly, joining Simon at the table. "Since when can women only be interested in sports because of a man?"

Simon laughed. "Sorry. Frankly, you don't seem like the basketball type. And a Jazz fan? They're way out of first place."

"You've been in the jungle too long! They're in first place in the Midwest Division, and last year they took the Houston Rockets to seven games in the playoffs. So watch what you say!" she warned. "This could be the year they go all the way to the finals. Anyway, I'm no fair weather fan."

"Obviously, if you drive in to see them in the winter. But do you honestly think they have a chance this year?" He still looked skeptical.

"Do you want lunch?"

Simon nodded.

"Then not another negative word about my team, or you go hungry," she threatened. Getting a clean cup, she poured what seemed like her tenth cup of cocoa today. At two hundred calories a cupful, she'd have a hard time fitting in her jeans.

"We'd better change the subject because I can't think of any thing positive. What about football?"

"You mean that game where you sit outside huddled under a blanket in freezing weather with snowflakes blinding you?"

"Yes."

"Not on my agenda! I suppose you love it?"

"The Forty-niners and Steve Young. Now that's who I plan on getting season tickets for."

"You're not a BYU fan?" she said scornfully.

"Not on your life," he defended himself vigorously.

Grasping his hand, Amanda leaned closer and said in a serious tone, as if giving him good advice. "Add warm-blooded to your list of wifely attributes." Not anticipating the rush of excitement his touch sent through her, she quickly dropped his hands. Warm but distant, that was her goal. This was too close, much too close.

"Hot-blooded and impetuous sounds even better!"

"It would! But do those types usually wear aprons?"

"Sure," he replied confidently, finishing his hot chocolate. He twirled the dial of the radio and faintly, they heard an announcer say, "A high pressure front is just moving into Washington, which should arrive in southern Idaho around three a.m. By ten o'clock tomorrow morning, the storm should be out over the plains states. We'll be days digging out from beneath this one. Southeast Idaho hasn't recorded this much snow since 1927. We're living history, folks…"

"Wonderful," Amanda said drily. "There are a number of other historical things I'd rather live through."

"Name one," Simon challenged.

Amanda thought and thought, unable to come up with one tangible idea. "My mind's blank. I think we've been stranded here so long my mind's turned to mush."

"More like slush!" he amended with a laugh.

Amanda rolled her eyes in disgust.

"…the transformer part will be airlifted in and should arrive early tomorrow morning. The power company estimates electricity should be back on by mid-morning…"

"And then the others should be able to leave Salt Lake," Amanda said. "Why don't you check the phone and see if we can get through to them."

Simon went over to the phone and listened for a minute, before clicking the receiver a couple of times. "We're still cut off from civilization."

"At least the end is in sight!" Thank goodness. Today had gone remarkably smoothly, but she didn't want to take any chances on anything else happening, like the kerosene lamp episode.

Feeling like a kitchen drudge, Amanda floured the chicken and started lunch. By the time she had the dinner ready, Simon had the table set. After they'd finished the dishes, Simon said, "Anything to read around here, besides your column?"

Amanda laughed. "Let's check the den." She hadn't seen anything upstairs, although she hadn't checked Simon's bedroom or the main bathroom which had crossed her up last time.

Next to a hide-a-bed were floor-to-ceiling bookshelves. "You're in luck. Here's Louis L'Amour." Ben must love him, because there was an entire shelf of them. On the other hand, Jenny didn't appear to read much because Amanda didn't see any other fiction. Of course, when would she find the opportunity?

Canning food and living in a nineteenth-century home probably didn't leave much free time, and now with a new baby... She shook her head. Jenny's lifestyle left a lot to be desired in her estimation.

"Don't tell me you're a Louis L'Amour lover, too?"

Actually she'd never read one, but she could hardly admit it. "Oh sure."

Simon scanned the books on the other shelves. "I'm surprised there aren't any mysteries."

"I seldom have time to read here."

"What do you do in the evening? I don't see a TV set."

What did Jenny do? Amanda hadn't seen evidences of handiwork or crafts. But then, her cursory inspection of the house hadn't revealed Jenny and Ben in any great depth. Her eyes caught on a pile of magazines on the floor next to the desk. "Read magazines. It helps to keep track of the competition." She crossed the small room and picked up the entire pile. Oh, wonderful. Men's magazines. *Field and Stream, BYU Sports, Car and Driver, Readers Digest.* Flipping through them she got a clear picture of Jenny's husband—a car-loving fisherman who liked BYU sports.

After checking the various books, Simon selected one and said, "I'm all set. What about you?"

"Me too," she answered as she sat on the floor, leaning against the sofa. Absorbing the warmth of the fire, she flipped through the pages of the first magazine while Simon pulled a chair closer to the fire. The best fishing spots in the West, pictures of trophy trout, the latest fishing equipment, and guns. Nothing appealed to her, so she picked up *Reader's Digest*.

"What's Your Mating IQ?" was emblazoned across the cover. Now that sounded intriguing. Turning to page 65, she found a quiz. Mark A, B, or C. Add up the points. That was simple enough. *1. Which do you notice first when you meet a woman?*

She began to laugh aloud as she scanned the rest of the questions. "Simon, do you want to find out your type?"

"Type of what?" He looked up blankly.

"Type of wife. What else is important?"

"Somehow I'm beginning to get suspicious of your eagerness to marry me off." He eyed her suspiciously and laid down his book. "Do you know something I don't?"

"Just answer the questions. What do you notice first when you meet a woman? A. Her looks. B. Her mind. C. Her personality."

"None of the above. Her smile."

"There isn't a none-of-the-above, so what's your next choice?"

"Mind."

"Give yourself one point."

After the next two questions, Simon had a total of seven points.

"Number four. Where would you take a woman on your first date? A. To see professional sports. B. To dinner and the symphony. C. To your apartment for an intimate dinner for two."

"C. To my apartment for an intimate dinner." He grinned at her.

"You buy the groceries and ask her to cook. Right?"

"If she's Laura Reynolds or a reasonable facsimile. Otherwise I prefer not to risk ptomaine."

"Wow! That answer was worth seven points. You're cooking now!"

He groaned at the pun.

"Where would you spend your honeymoon? A. An expensive hotel in New York City. B. A grass shack in Tahiti. C. Hiking the Appalachian Trail."

"Cross out B immediately. Probably A."

"Now why would you want to get the poor girl used to the good life?" She grinned knowingly at him. "On the other hand, you might want to give her a little romance before her life of drudgery begins."

"Don't worry about the romance," he said firmly, "that won't be a problem." Dark blue eyes met green ones, and the intensity of his drew her to him. She felt caught by the lure he unwittingly cast. Stop! She broke the spell. The problem was she was beginning to worry about romance—hers. Here was a perfectly wonderful man who interested her on all levels, and she was helpless to do anything about it.

"I'm not," she said, reaching for a pillow to cushion her back. "It's the drudgery that worries me! You get three points for that answer. The grass shack scored seven. Too bad you're not more imaginative."

"I'll take my chances with the score. How many more of these half-baked questions are there?"

"One. You know how these magazines are. They want an in-depth analysis. Now listen carefully. You are attracted to women who A. Are witty. B. Defer to your judgment. C. Have a Mona Lisa smile and are silent."

Amanda paused and continued before he could speak, "It seems to be a toss-up though I can't see much difference in deferring to your judgment and being silent. So, do you want someone clinging to you verbally or just clinging."

"It doesn't matter. I just like the idea of clinging." Unfortunately, in this forced confinement with Laura Reynolds, Simon was beginning to visualize her clinging to him. What was he thinking? He'd obviously been in the jungle too long. Married women had never appealed to him. And yet he found himself attracted to Laura Reynolds.

Unfortunately, by coming here practically straight from the jungle, he hadn't had a chance to become acclimated to civilization again, let alone women. When he'd read Laura Reynolds's article, he had no idea what the woman was like. The mischievous gleam in her green eyes made them glitter like jewels—in the perfect setting of her golden polished face and sun-streaked hair. *She's married*, he reminded himself for what seemed like the fifteenth time.

He shook himself out of his reverie in time to hear her say, "Mona Lisa might not say anything; she'd just refuse to do it. So let's give you a woman who will meekly defer to your judgment. That's worth two points." She quickly added up the points. "You have a total of eighteen. Now for the explanation. Sixteen to twenty-one points. You are a dull, run-of-the-mill, humdrum person who will be happiest married to someone with little imagination who is content to let you be the boss and never leave the suburbs. You—"

"You're making that up!"

Before Amanda could move out of the way, Simon snatched the magazine from her and began reading, "Sixteen to twenty-one points. You are an average man. Occasionally you will do something different to add a little spice to your life, but on the whole you prefer routine and order—" He tossed the magazine back to her. "This is as bad as what you made up. Great Scott! Routine and order!"

Amanda suppressed a smile. "Frankly, I thought it was a perfect description. Isn't that what makes good bankers?"

"I prefer," he said firmly, "imaginative risk-takers."

"You've got to be kidding. Somewhere you've got that mixed up with venture capitalists."

He looked disgusted. Then glancing at the magazines she was holding he said, "These are the competition? Since when did *Today's Home* start test driving cars, or giving fishing hints?"

"To be perfectly honest, these aren't what I read in the evenings." Not a chance. "In town I read the competition, and I prefer magazines that are mentally stimulating." She grinned.

He raised his eyebrows skeptically. "Do you actually consider recipes and furniture arranging mentally stimulating?"

"It depends on your perspective. They stimulate my mind to think of new ideas. I'm usually too busy writing and testing new ideas to do much reading out here."

He glanced at the magazine still in her hand. "What kind of men did you date before Rob?" Simon looked extremely interested.

Great! A chance to actually be herself, not Laura Reynolds. "Actually while I was in college I dated a lot of jocks, whose minds were strictly on the next game—and being seen with a

UCLA songleader—me. When I moved to New York I went out with lawyers, accountants, politicians, ed—"

"Politicians? Anyone I know?"

She laughed. "Not unless you know the borough presidents. I read an article on how to meet men. One of the ways was to join political campaigns. So I did. And the article was right. I went out with quite a few I met that way. Mostly campaign workers. But they were serious types, a lot of them driven to succeed." Like Brett. "After a while I got tired of licking envelopes and bringing bean dip to victory parties, so I haven't done it the last couple of..."

Amanda looked at Simon. His raised eyebrows told her that he'd noticed. It was her worst mistake in two days and she did it to herself. One more word and she'd have dug a pit she wouldn't have been able to get out of. *Distant*, she reminded herself. *Stay cool and distant.*

She forced herself to meet his eyes and give a careless shrug. "Needless to say it was before I met Rob." Way before, since their first meeting wasn't scheduled to take place for thirty-six hours. So it wasn't really a lie, she consoled herself.

Simon nodded his head understandingly, and she relaxed slightly and laid the magazine down. "What about you? What kind of women do you date?" Then she couldn't resist adding, "Besides Home Ec majors?"

He laughed. "Home Ec majors weren't even in my vocabulary while I was at Harvard. I wasn't a jock, but I did like to be seen with songleader types."

There was that smile again! She had to resist. Thankfully, Simon went on.

"While I was getting my MBA at Wharton, I was too busy to date much. Once I started working for the bank, I was mature enough to be able to appreciate more in a woman than her looks. I knew a number of women in the diplomatic corps, but no serious relationships." Enough about him. He was interested in Laura. "Where did you meet Rob?"

She could hardly say Spindrift Farm, she replied airily, "At a Save-the-Whales rally."

"You're kidding!" Every time Laura opened her mouth, Simon was more surprised. He just couldn't fathom her being interested in wildlife causes. But he found this side of her intriguing. From looking at her he would never expect such depth. With every hour she became more complex.

"I'm not!" Actually it was a cause that she was passionately interested in. "Do you realize that where once there were two hundred thousand blue whales in the Southern Hemisphere, now there are less than five hundred left? They're on the verge of extinction."

"No I didn't. But even more importantly, just what kind of men go to Save-the-Whales rallies?" This Rob must be really something—a writer, a farmer, a Save-the-Whales advocate. What couldn't he do? Simon was all the more anxious to meet him. Rob was obviously as fascinating as his wife.

"Very interesting ones!" If only you knew, Amanda said silently. They had been interesting all right, but hardly husband material unless bearded zealots appealed to you.

"Laura, you constantly surprise me!" He was having a difficult time reconciling this new Laura to the one he thought he knew: cook extraordinaire. Songleader he could believe, but sea-life activist? "With your looks and sense of style, I'm surprised you didn't want to be an actress."

Giving him a rueful glance, she said, "I thought I wanted to be one until I realized nobody was going to pluck me off a stool at the corner drugstore and say 'I vant to make you a star.' I don't take rejection well, and going to audition after audition with a million women more beautiful than I was didn't appeal to me."

"And there isn't rejection in writing?"

"Tons of it. But you're not being rejected personally because you're 5'8" and blonde, instead of 5'4" and brunette."

"Sounds logical."

She laughed. "Just what I would expect you to say. Isn't that one of the words from the quiz describing you?"

He grimaced. "That quiz was enough to turn me off men's magazines for life."

"Heavens, I didn't mean to scar your psyche."

"Rest assured it hasn't been."

Amanda had been joking, but Simon gave her the impression that he was quite comfortable with who he was, wherever he was and whatever he was doing. He had the confidence to carry off whatever he chose to do, be it dishes or chopping wood.

Today turned out well, Amanda thought, savoring a pleasant sense of accomplishment as she spread her blankets in front of the fire and crawled into them.

The fire crackled with the spitting of hot sap. As he had the previous night, Simon lay with his head barely six inches from her head, but Amanda realized that tonight was different. They'd spent the last two nights in exactly these same positions, but tonight he was no longer a stranger. Now he was a friend, Amanda realized with wonder.

This was a totally different intimacy. The last two days were a kind of sharing that she'd never experienced before. Not with her parents. Not with her girlfriends. Certainly not with Brett. Someone to talk to, someone supportive. Someone witty and fun to be around. A man liberated enough to share the chores. Never in her best nightmares would she have imagined that being stranded in the snow could be so pleasant. Still the edginess persisted and she didn't know if it was Simon himself or fear of being found out.

"Simon?"

"Hmmmm?" His voice was warm and drowsy.

"Did I wake you?"

"No. I was just lying here staring at the fire, thinking how different this Christmas is from last."

"I bet you never dreamed of this."

"No, I dreamed of other things."

Amanda could tell from the tone of his voice that this was deeply personal to him.

"I'd be lying if I said I didn't enjoy my life just the way it was. My motto was 'He travels fastest who travels alone.' So I never even entertained the thought of marrying. But marriage looks pretty good to me now."

"You may have difficulty finding someone who loves the city, but only wants to cook and do housework." She cocked her head. "You could try a maid service."

He laughed. "Oh, we might stray as far as the suburbs. But we'll live in the same house the rest of our lives, so our children will have a feeling of stability."

"You're living in the past. Haven't you heard? We live in a mobile society. As a matter-of-fact, I always looked forward to my father's transfers. There would be new people to meet and new places to discover."

"And you'd be the new kid in the school again, trying to fit into the group."

"So what? After I did fit in, I had added five or ten names to my address book. I used to get letters almost every day from friends I'd left, or who had gone somewhere else when their fathers were transferred."

"Not everyone is as adaptable as you obviously were."

"Not everyone had parents like mine who conscientiously made sure I knew what was important and what was not."

Sighing, as though trying to equate that with his own experience, he shook his head. "Maybe, but I guess it's all academic now. I'm planning to settle down, settle in and never leave the continental U.S. again. I'll never give rebels another chance at me."

"You'll be bored," she warned, tilting her head to look at him in the firelight.

"I think for someone who advances the country lifestyle the way you do, you have some conflicting prejudices."

She'd forgotten, again! "Not at all. I'd never try to convert someone to farm life. I'm just saying that being the daughter of a diplomat wasn't a bad way to grow up, and I think a family can be happy anywhere, as long as they're together."

"True. I just believe that a family can be more together if they have a permanent home."

"I'm going to give you that one and concede the argument. You're welcome to create any kind of home you want for your family. When you finally have a family of your own."

"Thank you. And with any luck the home would be just like Spindrift Farm."

Turning over on her back, Amanda watched the shadows flicker across the ceiling. Sharing her thoughts with Simon made her realize how much she wanted someone like him. Someone with roots, with dreams and aspirations, with integrity. Someone she could respect.

Someone like Simon. But at this point, she thought wearily, she saw little chance of it happening.

Chapter 8

Letter from Spindrift Farm—

How wonderful it is to live on a farm with large stands of timber. In the summer we have the primeval feeling of Early America. The trees shade the land and cleanse the atmosphere. On our hikes we watch for trees that might provide just the touch we want for Christmas. In the winter we search for the perfect one. One we've grown on our land and have watched from the time it was a seedling.

The shrill ringing of the phone pierced the stillness. Amanda woke with a start. Throwing the covers back and rolling onto her side, she got to her feet and stumbled to the phone.

"Hello?"

"Amanda? Are you okay?"

It was Becki. The phone was working! Amanda leaned back against the wall and closed her eyes. Her heart pounded as if she'd just run the 100-yard dash. No matter what time it was, it was too early.

"How are things going?"

"Fine. If you don't mind no electricity, no phone, no heat except for the fireplace, and only chicken to eat."

"Nothing's happened to blow it, has it?" Becki asked anxiously. "It's only been three days!"

"Never say "only" three days! So far so good—but I've had some *very* close calls," Amanda whispered.

"Good," Becki sounded pleased. "Is it still snowing there?"

"I don't know. I haven't looked outside yet today. Without any power we've been forced to sleep by the fireplace."

"Sleeping with him in front of the fireplace doesn't sound too wise," Becki cautioned.

"You sound like my mother. There wasn't an alternative short of freezing to death. Any idea how long before you'll be leaving?"

"Ah, now, that's the problem," Becki said ruefully. "The roads are still closed from Sardine Canyon on. Conditions should be better by this afternoon, but don't hold your breath."

"This afternoon?" Wonderful. Maybe she could just hold out that long.

"At the earliest. Otherwise, tomorrow."

"Tell Paul to make it today." After all, she was still in charge of this project.

Simon appeared in the doorway and slanted a look in her direction before opening the stove. He wondered if it were Rob on the phone. Laura sounded upset.

Amanda pulled the irritation she felt into an expression, she hoped, of regret.

"Well, I'm terribly disappointed, darling, but don't even try to come until you know it will be safe."

"I take it you can't talk."

"I love you, too. Bye now."

"Way to go!"

Amanda dropped the receiver on the hook and crossed the room to look out the window. The sky was still overcast, but only a few snowflakes drifted by. "Good news! No snow!" She felt like cheering! "Have you ever had better news?"

"Oh yes," he said definitely. "Two weeks ago—or simply put, a lifetime ago—when the missionaries said they had a short-wave radio!" Actually, this ran a close second. He wanted Rob around as a constant reminder that Laura was married.

"I'm sorry," her voice was penitent. "I know this seems paltry beside that. How come the missionaries were out in the jungle?"

Simon didn't mind talking about this part of the experience. "These particular ones were led by a remarkable woman whose husband had been killed by headhunters. She went back to live among the tribe, to bring Christianity to them. She kept in contact with the district police and the outside world by radio."

"She wasn't afraid for her own life?"

"No, she felt her work was a calling from God, and with Him by her side, she was fearless."

"What faith! I had a friend once who trained to be a Baptist missionary in the mountain region of the Philippines. As part of her training, she and the others would be awakened at night to go on long hikes and weren't allowed to take any water. Her stories were fascinating, but I can't say I'd like to change places. Give me the city any day."

"Are you kidding? I can't imagine Laura Reynolds anywhere but Spindrift Farm." Actually he could. His first impression had been 'this ain't no Betty Crocker,' but it had grown less difficult to believe that the charming and talented woman across from him was the same person that appeared on the inside flap of her book. Except for the occasional jarring note, as when she seemed to catch herself and look at him with a startled, almost frightened expression on her face, like right now. But the expression on her face—

Changed immediately to a mischievous grin. "Just kidding," she teased."I wanted to see the look on your face when I said it."

Her sudden transformation left Simon slightly bewildered, but he managed to ask, "Was that Rob on the phone?"

She nodded. "He said the roads are still closed, and he doesn't know when they will be able to get away."

"Tomorrow?"

"Maybe today!" He could tell she was excited to see her husband again, and felt a twinge of something. *She's a married woman.* He found that the words were becoming a steady refrain.

"I know you'll really be glad when he gets here." He'd be glad too. Although they had been careful to observe all the proprieties, being here alone with Laura was getting to be more and more like playing house. And the last thing he wanted to do was play house with a married woman. If he were going to maintain any distance, they needed to be outside. No more intimate card and Scrabble games. "After breakfast why don't we unload your car?"

"Sounds like a good idea." Maybe they were going to get this show on the road at last. Amanda flipped the light switch a couple of times to no avail. "We still don't have power."

"Just be grateful it's stopped snowing. I'll put some water on, and you can have the kitchen first."

Running up the stairs to the bedroom, she felt like she'd been released from prison. Relief was at hand. Even the sight of her frizzy hair couldn't quell her elation, and she quickly twisted her hair up on her head, donning blue cords and a matching blue velour sweater. By the time she'd returned, the water was warm and she washed up. Once she had her makeup on, Amanda felt as if she could face anything the day produced.

An hour later, they'd finished breakfast and were ready to tackle the car. The wind had blown the snow into six-foot drifts against the fences, but surprisingly enough there was a trough through the middle of the driveway. Picking up a snow shovel and the broom, they cleaned off the porch.

Amanda squinted her eyes against the glistening snow. "Is this the same world we experienced the last three days? It seems impossible."

"I forgot winter could be this beautiful," Simon said, sitting down on the cold steps. He didn't want to admit it to Laura, but he seriously doubted he had the strength to do the entire lane. "The air is so clean and clear, I can taste it."

She joined him on the steps. "It is, isn't it?" Her voice filled with awe. "Like the songs. It's no wonder people make such a big deal out of a white Christmas."

When they started down the lane, Amanda felt as if she were

in another world. The branches of the trees were heavily laden with snow, and they draped over the path, giving the area the feeling of an ice cave. She felt completely isolated from reality, as if she had been thrust into another dimension, a fantasy realm. The drifts and trees shielded them from the slight drizzle of snow, and the only sounds were those of Simon's shovel and their labored breathing.

Leaning on his shovel to rest, Simon said, "Do you think we've been transported to the nether world?"

"And sentenced to hard labor." Panting from the exertion, Amanda stopped sweeping. "Is this trip worth it?"

"Don't tell me after all this exertion, there's even a question that we might be working for naught?"

"There isn't," she reassured, and started to sweep again.

But when they finally had the car uncovered, they took another break. "It almost seems too bad we cut that path through the snow. We've destroyed the clean sweep the wind gave it and now it's reduced to looking like any other shoveled lane," Simon said regretfully, looking at the evidence of their work.

"Since it was between the beauties of nature outside and life as we're used to living it inside, we didn't have much choice."

"Yeah. Ready to go again?"

Amanda unloaded the back seat and carefully stacked boxes in Simon's arms. Then she picked up an unwieldy but lightweight box to carry herself. After the third trip, they both collapsed on the couch to recuperate.

"That was a job, I'm glad is over," Simon said, pulling off his gloves. He was surprised at the toll his imprisonment had taken on his stamina. Only sheer determination had gotten him through the last hour.

When she'd caught her breath, Amanda said, "If you thought that was bad, you should try doing it all by yourself."

Simon looked at her strangely. "Did you load the car all by yourself?"

Not again! Now he wonders where dear old Rob was. "Yes.

Rob was tied up. So I made a dozen trips from the apartment to the car."

"After all that work, I'm surprised you could even be civil to me when I showed up."

"It was easy." Now it is. At the time it wasn't. Amanda could hardly believe she'd known Simon for only three days. It seemed like forever.

A half hour later when Simon opened the boxes of greenery, Amanda realized she was on thin ice again. She should have known the fir trees surrounding the farm were a ready resource.

Simon peeked into one box. "Wreaths?" he asked in surprise. "A little like carrying coals to Newcastle, isn't it?"

"A little, but I decided in the interest of time to buy them this year."

"That makes sense. You had enough things listed in your column to take a month, and we've only got four days left."

"And if the others don't get here soon with the rest of our supplies, we won't even have that long."

Simon looked shocked. "You mean there's more?"

Amanda just shook her head in resignation.

By noon glimpses of a watery sun were beginning to emerge from the cloud cover. Amanda hoped that by afternoon the sky would be clear. Of course it meant a hard freeze during the night, so no telling when the roads would actually be open. In the meantime, they needed to get started on "Christmas at Spindrift Farm."

"Do you feel up to cutting a Christmas tree?" Amanda asked, as she finished unpacking the last box and putting her Christmas gifts on the dining room table.

Simon, who had just picked up his Louis L'Amour book, looked up at her. "Isn't that something you'd rather wait to do when Rob gets here?"

She hesitated for a split second. What would the real Laura and Rob do? "No, tramping around in the woods while I find the perfect tree doesn't particularly appeal to him. Sometimes we've spent a whole day out looking, so it's not his favorite activity." Her granddad did it just because Nonnie loved it so much.

A look of pleasure rippled across Simon's face, giving him a boyish appeal. "It sounds like a great idea to me. It reminds me of home." For a moment he seemed pensive, then seeming to shake off his feelings, he laid his book down.

They bundled up again and ventured outdoors, pulling the sled behind them that Amanda, with some quick thinking, had found in the garage. Looking at the deep snow across the meadow, Amanda said doubtfully, "Maybe it wasn't such a good idea to go after the tree today. I don't feel like any more shoveling, do you?"

"No, but it shouldn't be as deep once we get to the woods."

They struggled through the thigh-high snow across the large field that separated the house from the woods. "Growing up we always went to the mountains the day after Thanksgiving and chose our Christmas tree." His words came in short bursts. "It was a major project and we spent the entire day tramping up and down the hills, hunting for trees and then picnicking in the snow."

Low hills circled the homesite, and when they entered the woods, they started climbing. The branches of the trees had kept the snow from accumulating as deep here, which was a welcome relief to Amanda. But the trees also cut off the warmth of the sun. She found that toiling through the snow took so much effort she didn't feel any colder.

"This is harder than I thought it would be," Amanda said, holding her side as a sharp pain shot through it.

"Actually, either I'm out of condition or not as young as I used to be, because this is harder than I remember," Simon remarked as he stopped to catch his breath.

"Want to turn back?" She was all for cutting down a tree, any tree, and going home.

"Never! We're after the perfect tree. Remember? Perfect trees were hard to find even when I was a kid."

If she had stopped to think, she would have remembered how hard it was to find the perfect tree on a tree lot, so why had she imagined a forest would be any different. She also hadn't counted on all the climbing. But she could hardly tell Simon that. She couldn't admit she was a novice. If her dad had only been posted to a Scandinavian country, maybe she would have had the experience! Or if, she thought ruefully, she had ever joined her grandparents on one of their pilgrimages to the woods.

"Well?"

Hastily, she said, "Uh…I'm out of condition. I've spent too much time cooking and writing lately."

"I know what you mean, pacing around a grass hut has left me sadly out of shape." He hated to admit it, but much more, and Laura would be pulling him home on the sled.

He was relieved when she said, "Let's try in that direction." She pointed to the side, not up. If they could have had neat, well-groomed paths instead of deep snow to plow through, the hike would have been easier. He smothered a groan. What a wimp he'd become.

But all-in-all Amanda was having a much better time than she'd expected. Even though the air was cold and the snow wet, she couldn't remember a more dazzling day. Maybe she'd always given winter short shrift. But then she remembered the blizzard of the last couple of days, the lack of electricity, and decided she'd still take the Caribbean.

"How about this one?" He'd asked that question so many times without having found a serious contender that Amanda just kept going.

Suddenly a great glob of wet snow hit her on the shoulder, sending sprays of it into her hair and against her neck.

Ducking down, she scooped up a handful of snow, shaping it into a ball as she turned, and heaved back in Simon's general direction. Of course it missed. That's what happened when a person hadn't thrown a snowball since elementary school.

She saw the next one coming, and trying to jump out of the

way in the deep snow, she lost her balance. Laughing, she lay in the hole her body had made in the snow and stared at the sky. Not a single cloud anywhere. In the periphery of her vision the deep green of the pines stretched endlessly upward, and somewhere a winter bird was singing for joy. It had to be for joy. Even as tired as she was, the day was too splendid for anything else.

"Here." Standing above her, Simon reached down his hand. He was grinning, an expression of satisfaction on his face and sparkling in his eyes.

"I'm stuck."

His rich, mellow chuckle floated away to join the song of the bird. He bent over, extending his hand still closer, and she reached up with both of hers to grab it. As soon as she had a firm grip, she yanked as hard as she could, rolling out of the way at the same time.

He landed face first in the snow. Still laughing, he twisted onto his side and shook his fist at her. "All I wanted to do was show you the perfect tree."

Before she could answer, he scrambled to his feet, hauled her upright, and marched her back the way he'd come. "See?"

It was perfect. The most beautiful tree Amanda had ever seen. Its color was dark and vibrant, just exactly the color a Christmas tree should be. From the bottom to the very top, each branch seemed to have been put in place by a perfectionist. In her mind's eye, she decorated it with the things they'd make and knew they couldn't possibly do better.

"I'll take it." She turned to smile at Simon and for a moment they stared at each other while something almost tangible passed between them. Then Simon laughed, breaking the spell, and turned toward the sled for the axe.

The tree was about ten feet tall, and to Simon's disgust, he had little power in his swing. After what seemed like an age and a half, the tree finally fell over. Together they picked up the tree, positioned it on the sled, and anchored it down with the strap.

"You pull and I'll make sure it doesn't fall off," Amanda offered.

They turned to go down the hill. With her hand holding the tree, they avoided being run down by the sled. Almost giddy with happiness, Amanda began to sing "Jingle Bells" and Simon joined in.

They'd just finished when they heard a snowmobile come over the hill behind them. Simon turned, raising his eyebrows questioningly, and Amanda lifted her shoulders in response.

The machine pulled up next to them, and when the rider got off, she could see he wore a National Forest Service uniform. "Pardon me, ma'am, sir," he said, polite but firm. "Could I see your permit for that tree?"

"What?" Becki had said nothing about needing a permit to cut a tree on her brother's farm. But how could she explain that to the ranger with Simon standing right there?

"Your permit for cutting a tree on federal land."

"We aren't on federal land," she said, equally firm, determined not to be cowed by this man just because he wore a uniform.

"The boundary of Caribou National Forest runs right along that ridge. You're about a quarter of a mile inside."

Taking a deep breath, Amanda looked the ranger straight in the eye and said solemnly, "Then I guess you'll have to jail us, because we don't have a permit."

Simon made a growling kind of noise which she thought was probably a laugh caught in the act of trying to escape.

The ranger heard it too and grinned at her. "We don't jail people. But we do issue fines. Three-hundred-dollar fines." He pulled a narrow notebook out of his inside jacket pocket and looked at Simon. "Your name please."

"He's my guest," Amanda said quickly. "Make the ticket out to me."

"Whatever you say. Your name please."

"Uh-h…Laura Reynolds." Of course, giving an assumed name might only make the situation worse, but she didn't want

Simon to be stuck with a three-hundred-dollar fine.

"Address?"

For a second she considered giving her Salt Lake address, then decided she might as well be hung for a sheep as a goat. "Spindrift Farm."

The ranger lowered his notebook and looked at her. "Say, are you the woman who writes those magazine articles?"

"Yes, I am." And while she was at it, she might as well get hung for the whole flock.

"My wife reads your column, and she loves it. In fact, she tries all your recipes. For Christmas she's making your chestnut stuffing."

Amanda smiled graciously and thanked him. "I'd love to hear how it turns out. Tell her to write me a note in care of the magazine. Hearing from readers is one of the best parts of my job."

"Boy, is she going to be surprised when I tell her you were caught stealing a tree."

"Do you have to mention it?" Amanda said dryly, and Simon chuckled again.

"This is the most interesting day I've had in a long time," the ranger said. He finished filling out the form and tore off the top copy for her. "You have a week to pay this."

"Thanks for being so understanding. I really didn't know we'd wandered off the farm."

His brow furrowed. "Spindrift Farm is near here? I thought I knew all the farms in this area."

"Fairly close," Amanda said, decisively, hoping he'd leave it at that.

"Where? I'd like to point it out to my wife. She'll be thrilled."

Amanda hesitated, feeling trapped.

"It's four miles this side of town on the main highway," Simon said helpfully.

"Drop by, I'd love to meet her." Amanda gave him a weak smile and crossed her fingers. The last thing she wanted to do was meet one of Laura Reynolds's eager fans out here.

The ranger looked amazed. "You're serious?"

She forced herself to say heartily. "Certainly. Christmas isn't Christmas without friends dropping in." Under normal circumstances, that is although these couldn't be called normal circumstances by any stretch of the imagination. She felt forced to be extra hospitable with Simon hanging on every word. "Merry Christmas."

"Merry Christmas," Simon echoed.

After the ranger remounted the snowmobile and plowed his way back into the woods, Amanda turned to Simon. "You'd think he would have better things to do than drive around hunting for people cutting trees."

"At three hundred dollars a whack. I doubt there's a much better way to spend a winter day," Simon said, his eyes merry but his voice even. "In the future you should scout out your tree in advance. With a map."

"I'm absolutely certain that I'll never find myself in this situation again," Amanda told him with conviction.

Chapter 9

Letter from Spindrift Farm—

> *I never realized what a difference fresh ingredients make in cooking until I moved to the farm and started raising my own chickens. Large fresh eggs add immeasurably to the success of my Christmas baking.*

As soon as they emerged from the woods, Amanda could see that Becki and the others hadn't arrived. Simon's was the only car in front of the house, and hers was still stuck in the ditch. She tried to accept her fate with equanimity: she seemed to be handling the situation just fine on her own. But there had already been too many close calls.

"Where should we put the tree?" Simon asked when they got to the house.

"Let's shake the snow off and leave it on the porch until it dries off a little."

"Shouldn't we put the cut end in water?"

Since Simon sounded as if he knew all about it, she nodded her agreement. "You're right. Let me see if I can find a bucket. I guess my mind's somewhere else." Like in Salt Lake with her reinforcements.

"I'm sure you're worried about Rob getting here."

It seemed ironic that Simon should make the deception easier.

"I'm sure he wouldn't have left the city until the roads were clear, but certainly they've been clear long enough now for them." She hoped they'd left the very second it seemed likely they could make it.

"Hold onto the tree while I get something to put it in." Amanda checked the utility porch first and decided Jenny Canfield must be the most wonderful woman in the world. Two galvanized buckets stood next to the washing machine, one inside the other. She took the top one and hurried back to Simon.

"My dad used to use one just like this," Simon said, pushing the tree into her hand and taking the bucket. "He would fill it with wet sand and anchor the tree in it. That way the tree would stay fresh through the entire holidays."Amanda nodded her agreement.

"I guess if we fill this with snow it will do until we get ready to put the tree in the house," he continued.

"I have a regular Christmas-tree stand—the commercial kind that holds water, since sand seems unavailable this year."

Simon filled the bucket with snow and Amanda helped him set the tree in it. Then they went into the house to change out of their wet clothes.

She tried the light switch as she stepped into the kitchen.

"Civilization!" she said as the light flashed on. "I'll never take it for granted again." This meant they could sleep in the bedrooms and take a bath.

Although the water was tepid and the air cold, Amanda luxuriated in the feel of the shower water washing over her body. Amazing what shampoo, a blow dryer, and a crimper could do to enhance one's looks, she thought, looking at her reflection in the mirror. Amanda put on another pair of jeans and a heavy sweater. By the time she was back downstairs, she felt warm and normal and ready to face anything.

Simon was crouched in front of the fireplace, poking at the

coals. Outside the sun had fallen to just above the horizon. Since it wasn't quite 4:30, Becki might still make it.

"Are you hungry?" she asked.

"Starving." He pivoted on the balls of his feet and grinned at her. "There's something about run-ins with the law that whet the appetite."

"Especially when they let you walk away and you know you won't have to live on jailhouse food for three days."

"Or longer. Instead I know that Laura Reynolds, the best cook this side of the Mississippi, is going to feed me."

She dropped into the nearest chair and pulled up a footstool for her feet. "Only because you beat me at cards," she slanted him a grin, "by hook or by crook, and I suspect crook, and more importantly, because you like chicken!"

"Much more and I'll be clucking!"

"Don't look a gift horse in the mouth."

"You mean chicken in the craw," he retorted, his amusement obvious.

"Just so you get the point." The shower had restored her equanimity and she felt ready to tackle anything.

"What can I do to help?" he asked as he stood up.

"How are you at making chicken sandwiches?"

"It's been awhile, but I think I can manage." He reached down and pulled her up. "But what are you going to do?"

"I knew there was a snag in the plan. You mean I have to help?"

Simon pushed her into the kitchen. "You got it."

"I'll set the table and slice the fruitcake."

After they ate, Amanda glanced around the room, wondering what to do next. In the corner, she spied the box containing her nativity sets. "How would you like to hang some garlands and set out the manger scenes?"

"Good idea. I'll get the garlands." He headed for the back porch and Amanda followed him.

He swung the box up on his shoulder. "Where shall we start?"

"How about the bay window in the living room?"

He pulled out a long rope of pine branches and inhaled deeply. "Our first smell of Christmas."

"And my favorite," Amanda agreed enthusiastically. She might not choose to have a traditional tree, but she actually did love the smell of pine.

"Do you have a stepladder?" he asked. "I may be tall, but I still can't reach the top of some of these windows."

Amanda was silent for a moment. She couldn't remember seeing a stepladder anywhere. Finally, she said, "I think Rob's locked the ladder in the shed, so how about using the stool from the kitchen?"

"Okay. It isn't as high, but it will probably work as well."

When he returned with the stool, Amanda watched while he tried to reach the top of the window, missing it by several inches.

What next? She wished Becki would get here. At least she might know where the Canfields kept things.

"I think if I lean over this way and rest my foot on the window sill, I can reach it."

"We'll drape the garland over the curtain rod." The last thing Ben and Jenny needed was to come home and find nails pounded in around the windows.

"All set. Now if I can just keep my balance…"

Amanda, the greens swathed around her arms, reached up towards him, pulling the garland across her face and blinding herself. At that moment Simon reached down for the garland. Before Amanda knew what was happening, she found herself lying on the floor with her wind knocked out and Simon on top of her.

When he lifted his head, his lips, curved in an enticing little quirk, were only inches from her own. His mouth looked firm and wonderful, and his dark eyes gleamed. She knew without any doubt that she wanted him to kiss her. Tilting her head up towards him, she could feel her pulse race. As she felt her eyelids drift shut, she realized who she was. Laura Reynolds! While

Amanda Richards might be single and willing, Laura Reynolds certainly wasn't.

She sat up abruptly, pushing Simon onto the floor. "I've heard of fair maidens falling at the feet of knights in shining armor, but I didn't know it was ever vice versa." He had to have felt how much she'd wanted him to kiss her. Her cheeks heated with embarrassment. Of all the mistakes she'd made so far this was the worst, and she doubted either of them could gloss over it. But she'd try.

"And here I thought you'd done that on purpose." He stood up easily and held a hand down to her, pulling her up beside him. Simon pretended that their contact hadn't affected him. But it had. He was finding it harder and harder to be immune to her, and he wished that Rob would get here before he made a fool of himself.

"Invite a ton of bricks to fall on me?" she said lightly.

"Now I am insulted. Here I fell at your feet..."

"More like midsection."

"...and all you can do is complain."

She could read in his eyes that he wasn't complaining about the physical contact. What rotten luck! Why couldn't she just have met him somewhere else? Like at the bank when she opened her checking account.

"Are you afraid of heights? Or do you feel like trying again?"

"Standing on a two-and-a-half foot stool has never made me dizzy before. Maybe it's the force of your perfume. What are you wearing? Vanilla behind your ears?"

"Can you imagine Laura Reynolds wearing anything else?" she said primly, picking up the greenery.

"Probably not." He stood on the stool again and anchored his foot on the window sill. "Now just hold your arms as high as you can reach naturally. Let me do the rest."

Amanda held the garlands up, and Simon took them, carefully draping them over the curtain rods, making sure the sides were even. He stepped down. "What do you think?"

"Pretty good for an amateur."

Ignoring the potency of her grin, he said casually, "Who're you calling an amateur?"

"Don't worry, by the time we finish this you'll be a pro. Let's put the ends across the sill and nestle a nativity set in the center."

Amanda opened the box. Carefully wrapped in bubble pack were the nativity scenes she'd packed just to bring here for Simon Kent's Christmas. The first one was made of olive wood from Israel, given to her by her parents for her twenty-second birthday. Now every time they traveled to a new country, they picked up a nativity scene for her, and she treasured every one. Lovingly, she unwrapped a shepherd.

"What do you think? Isn't it beautiful?"

Simon joined her on the floor. Together they assembled the first set and placed it in the window.

"How many sets do you have?" he asked.

"Six. My parents have given them to me over the years."

He looked curious. "Why did you have them in town?" Comprehension slowly dawned on his face. "Oh, I recognize these. They were in this month's issue of *Today's Home*."

Actually they weren't, but now wasn't the time to set him straight. She just hoped he hadn't brought the magazine with him and compared them. "Here, why don't you put these in the window while I unwrap the others," she said.

Simon picked up the small figures and placed them among the greens. Stepping back to admire them, he said, "The polished wood has a simplicity about it that I like."

"It looks elegant all right. Let's put these brightly colored ones from Mexico on the coffee table."

After Simon arranged them on the table, he took a long garland from the box, and together they wound it around the banister from the second floor down to the front hallway.

Going into the kitchen, Amanda put some water on for hot chocolate. Then she hunted through the boxes to find the spools of red plaid ribbon. "Hold your hands out so I can wind the ribbon around them to make bows."

They made about a dozen bows and tied them to the railings. Then they swagged the mantle, putting a large bow in the center and one at each end.

"Let's put the large nativity set from Germany in the small kitchen fireplace." Amanda set the pieces back in the box and together they carried it into the kitchen.

"Any idea why they built two fireplaces?" Simon asked.

"Originally the small one was used to bake bread. They burned wood there until the bricks were heated. Then they removed the coals and baked their bread in it. The door's been removed." At least this was one thing she legitimately knew.

Carefully she took out the large figures and handed them to Simon, who arranged them in the oven. She wished she had straw to set them on, but she didn't mention that. If Becki knew where to locate some when she got here, they could add it later.

Amanda sighed. Life seemed so fraught with danger. She'd thought if she could just keep them decorating they'd make it through the evening. But then he'd fallen on her. Now any minute she expected to make another mistake so drastic that there would be no recovering from it. Like kissing Simon. What would he think of her? Amanda took another deep breath. Even though there had been a couple of close calls, everything was still under control—she hoped. She ignored the nagging little voice that kept asking, *But can you continue?*

"Why don't we start the tree next?" she asked. That should take several hours, and then it would be time to go to bed.

"Won't Rob mind?"

Darn Rob. Who needed a husband, anyway? Especially one that kept intruding at the most inopportune times. "Well, he might be a little disappointed, but we'd planned to do it tonight, and we're so far behind now that unless we do it, we'll never be able to do everything we'd planned with you."

He grinned, his eyes alight with expectations. "This is turning out to be one of the best Christmases of my life." Somewhere in the far reaches of his mind a voice kept reminding him that it wasn't only the Christmas customs that were enriching his stay. It was Laura Reynolds. Her charm, her wit, how easy she was to be with. And at last he was beginning to shake the anxious feeling of the last few months and feel safe again. He was glad to see that Laura was beginning to get past her nervousness around him.

"Why don't you go bring the tree in, and I'll find the box of lights." Amanda couldn't stop smiling as she looked at him. He was so full of zest and wonder, excited by the smallest, simplest gestures, and so easy to please. But, she cautioned herself, it would be dangerously easy to forget that he was an experienced world traveler with an acumen that made him the best at what he did, and which could serve him equally well in any situation. She must remember that this visit here was only a respite after months of captivity. And that uncanny knack for always asking the exact question that could trip her up. Won't Rob mind? Would a real husband mind? The trouble was, she knew her granddad, the Rob in Laura's column, *would* mind.

But how could she keep Simon occupied and entertained on an impersonal level if they didn't do the Christmasy things she'd brought for the whole crowd to do together? She would just have to avoid the intimacy that decorating the house created. No more dwelling on the fact that Simon was a handsome, unattached male. Even the drawn look on his face didn't diminish his attractiveness.

When Simon came in with the tree, Amanda had the box of decorations open. She took out the stand and placed it in front of the big bay window.

"Now lights." She had plenty of lights—tiny little white ones—enough to wind up the trunk and cover the branches.

"I always liked strings of different colored bulbs," Simon said reminiscently.

"Like your grandmother used?" she teased. He laughed and started stringing the lights on the higher branches. "Am I that transparent? Sometimes I think that jungle sun sent me back in time. It certainly made me reassess my priorities."

Working up from the bottom, Amanda tipped her head to look up at him. "You mean the past has become more meaningful than the present?"

He stopped tightening the lights in their sockets and looked at her. "No, but it's made me realize what I want my present to be. I spent a lot of time thinking about what I'd contributed to life, what I'd be remembered for. And the answer was always the same—not much. I realized I did want to leave something, and the most important thing in my life had always been my family. And at one time the Church. Unfortunately, both are still lacking in my life at the present. I decided if I ever got out of there, the first thing on my agenda was to get married, have my own family, and go back to church."

Church? She wondered if he were Catholic. Since he'd brought up the religion angle, she decided to ask him. "Are you Catholic?"

He looked perplexed. "No, why would you think that?"

Chagrined, she said, "The only people I know who say *the* Church are either Catholics or Mormons."

"Well, I'm a Mormon."

"Mormon!" She made no attempt to hide her amazement. "How on earth did you manage to keep that out of the papers when you were released? No matter what the deed, the press always adds parenthetically that someone is a Mormon."

"They didn't ask. I didn't tell." He cocked an eyebrow. "Does it make a difference?"

"No, of course not. I'm LDS myself. It surprised me that someone from Montana and an international banker to boot would be LDS."

"My great-grandfather was from Kimberly, Idaho. His brother-in-law was the agent for the Great Northern Railroad and they had some kind of program where they shipped a family and all their belongings free to Montana. In return, they leased them farm land. Being of pioneer stock, my grandparents, along with their five small children, took them up on the offer. They settled at Fort Shaw and eventually went into banking." He grinned at her. "I've just told you more than you ever wanted to know about my roots."

Smiling, Amanda shook her head. "No, but I do have a pertinent, or rather impertinent, question, whichever the case might be. Why didn't you go to the Y?"

"After Montana I wanted an Ivy League education and my grandfather, in particular, encouraged me." With a sly smile, he asked, "Why didn't you?"

"BYU wasn't known for its sun and surf."

He resumed tightening light bulbs. "What frivolity! Did you notice," he said piously, "my motives were of the highest—an excellent education, while yours were merely base—a desire to be a beach bum."

She laughed. "Not exactly accurate."

"Close enough!"

Amanda enjoyed the exchange. It had been a long time since she'd bantered with an attractive single man. And to think that he's a member of the Church!

"You sound as if you were particularly close to your grandparents."

"I was. My greatest hope at this point is that I will be able to instill the virtues they and my parents considered important in my children."

"I take it from what you said previously that you haven't been active in the Church."

"No. It was never a conscious decision. I just got busy and drifted into inactivity. In fact, I haven't given the Church much thought at all in recent years." He hesitated. He seldom revealed his innermost thoughts. But Laura Reynolds was different. He felt comfortable with her, as if he could tell her anything, and she'd understand. "While I was imprisoned, I questioned my beliefs. Did I really believe the Church was true? Was Joseph Smith actually a prophet?"

He stopped talking. Amanda did nothing to break the silence. The air was heavy with the emotion he felt.

He continued. "I started praying for the first time in years, and my questions were answered. I knew without a doubt that Joseph Smith was a true prophet and that he had restored the gospel." He paused again, Amanda thought, to gain control of his voice. "I also knew that I would be rescued."

Simon's deep personal revelations left Amanda with nothing to say that didn't seem to trivialize his experiences. Finally she said, "Did that make captivity easier?"

"I'd given up and felt fated to die there. Yes, it gave me hope. I knew if I could just hang on, help would come. Three weeks later some missionaries showed up. They had a shortwave radio."

"How long have your parents been gone?"

"During my senior year in college my parents were on their way to Mexico on vacation. My father was piloting a small plane which went down over the Wasatch Mountains. My grandfather passed away about five years ago, and my grandmother last year. She was eighty-seven." He nodded his head at the memory. "A wonderful woman, full of fire and vinegar to the end," he added softly. "Because of them, the Kent name stood for honesty and integrity."

"I think they've left you with a wonderful legacy to pass on."

"Thanks. Are you active in the Church?"

"Active and then some. I was just released as Beehive leader." She shook her head at the memory of all their activities.

Simon picked up more lights and carefully strung them between the green branches. "Do you and Rob want children?"

"Yes." For once she could just be herself and speak for Laura Reynolds also. "I've always wanted to be happily married and have several children. I never minded moving a lot while I was growing up, but I did mind being an only child. When I was nine, I decided to have ten kids. I could just visualize how wonderful a family that size would be. As I grew older, the number diminished, but I'd still like to be a mother."

Maybe it was the night, or Simon, but she found herself revealing things she'd never spoken aloud. "I guess I'm an instinctive nurturer."

"I agree. Everything from whales to strangers who need a feeling of stability to get them used to the real world again. How does Rob feel?"

"He agrees." What else could he do when she was making him up as she went along. She held out another string of lights to Simon.

"Spindrift Farm is a wonderful place to raise children."

"Yes." She was beginning to feel like she wouldn't mind having a farm like this someday. But one thing she'd insist on was an electric range.

"My prerequisite for a wife is that she be a homebody. Travel agents need not apply. In fact, Betty Crocker looks good to me—as does Laura Reynolds. Too bad you're taken!" Of course, she wasn't, but that made no difference. She wasn't Laura Reynolds nor was she a homebody. They were making slow work of the lights, and the way the conversation was heading, Amanda began to grow nervous.

"The lights are great. What are we putting on next?"

"Cranberry and popcorn ropes, felt ornaments we'll make ourselves, and decorated cookies." She straightened the last bulb. "And last but not least, our candy canes."

"Laura Reynolds," he reached out, and looking deep into her eyes, flicked her chin with his forefinger, "you are a wonderful person."

"Thank you," she said, feeling slightly numb. "I brought a batch of decorated cookies, so we can use those. And you can be in charge of popping the corn."

Amanda looked in the pantry for the oblong box of cookies. When they weren't there, she checked the cupboards. Finally, she turned to Simon. "Where did you put that flat box when we were unpacking? The one with the Christmas paper covering the outside?"

"I didn't see anything like that. Are you sure you brought it?"

"Positive." She tried to control the sinking feeling in the pit of her stomach. "You know that box I dropped in the snow? The cookies must have been in it."

"Well, we can make some more, can't we?"

"More sugar cookies?" The words came out unbidden, and then she felt like an idiot. Laura Reynolds wouldn't quell and quake at the idea of mixing up a batch of cookies. Neither would Amanda Richards, if they didn't have to be baked in a wood-burning stove and then decorated with a professional touch.

"Why not? Do we have anything better to do?"

Frankly she could think of several things better. But Laura Reynolds would never groan at the thought of whipping up a batch of cookies.

"What a good idea!" Amanda said cheerfully. "If you'll put the rest of this stuff away, I'll get out the ingredients." And find Nonnie's recipes. She'd included the ones from Laura's next year's book, *Christmas at Spindrift Farm*. She hoped the cookies would look as good as the pictures in the book, but she thought it was a rather vain hope.

Amanda laid the recipe on the counter and assembled bowl and beaters and measuring cups and spoons. Shortening, vanilla, flour. But no eggs anywhere. And no sugar. She checked the cupboard again. Nope. They'd used it all for the candy canes.

"Shortening?" Simon asked, startling her. He waved his hand over her assembled ingredients. "I thought Laura Reynolds would never settle for less than butter in her cookies."

Amanda thought quickly. "Butter makes the cookies too soft to hang on the tree. Unfortunately, we have a small problem. Since Rob was bringing the groceries, we don't have any eggs. I guess we'll have to wait until the others get here."

He looked perplexed. "I thought you raised chickens for fresh eggs."

Not that idiot column again! She crossed her fingers. "We've gotten rid of them, thank goodness. They'd never have survived the last few days." She hoped they wouldn't stumble onto a hen house filled with frozen chickens. But surely someone would have mentioned them before now.

"No problem. If the road has been plowed, we can just run down to the village and pick some up. Your car is probably still incapacitated, but mine should be running."

"Does your car have a snowblower attached to the front?" She looked skeptical. "Think of the lane."

He got up and looked out the window. "With a little more shoveling we can get out, and with snow tires we'll do just fine."

Then a new worry hit her. How would the clerks in the store react? They'd know she wasn't a native. She wished she could just send him to the store alone, but no, Laura Reynolds, perfect hostess, couldn't do that. She looked at Simon. He looked tired. "I refuse to let you go out after all the shoveling you've done. We invited you here to enjoy Christmas at Spindrift Farm, not work yourself to death."

Ignoring his protests, Amanda started to make more hot chocolate, but then she thought of the sparkling white grape juice. It was on the back porch and would certainly be chilled. "Since this is our last night alone at Spindrift Farm, why don't we relax in front of the fire and have some sparkling grape juice to celebrate our rescue?"

"A good idea."

"You go get comfortable, and I'll get it." On the top shelf of the last cupboard, Amanda found some goblets that made the drink more festive. Rinsing them off, she placed them on the tray and went for the juice. She would have liked to have had cheese and crackers, but since she didn't want to use up Paul's gift, she sliced some fruitcake instead.

The glow of the fire was the only light in the room, just the way it had been for the last three nights. But after their personal discussion Amanda knew the scene was too intimate. She set the tray on the lamp table and switched on the lamp. "Isn't it good to have enough light again." It sounded idiotic, but she couldn't risk her feelings.

Simon didn't comment, so Amanda filled their glasses. "To us," Simon said, touching her glass with his. "Survivors."

"Made possible only by your skill." She took a sip. "You will make someone a very fine husband. I know I've been giving you a hard time, but in spite of your traveling ways, I'm surprised someone hasn't snatched you up."

"I was always too fast on my feet to get caught. Now I'd like to come home to 'the little woman' who is standing at the door waiting in her apron, her cheeks dusted with flour."

"Since you're really serious about marriage, I suggest you don't mention your antiquated ideas until you've got a ring on her finger. Like I said before: no woman wants to be a drudge."

"The only thing I absolutely require is that she love to cook, and..." a roguish grin tugged at his lips, "don't worry, I'll make it worth her while."

Obviously it wouldn't have done Amanda any good to meet him in a bank. The minute Simon found out the status of her cooking, he'd have dumped her.

"All I ask is that she be another Laura Reynolds," he said expansively, as if he'd just paid her the supreme compliment.

Amanda grimaced. Laura Reynolds. That paragon of virtues was beginning to give her a pain. She'd much rather Simon would have said he wanted a tall woman with frizzed blond hair who looked good in pants. He hardly built her self-esteem with his last statement.

"Now, consummate cook, what's on the agenda for tomorrow?"

"First, we'll string the popcorn and cranberries. And with any luck at all, we'll have some help. Then we'll make the cookies."

At her reference to the others, Simon's expression darkened slightly. He felt as if he were waiting for the cavalry to arrive, and before they could get here, he'd have lost not only his scalp but his heart.

The next morning Amanda woke with a glow of happiness.

Her lips curled into a contented smile. Another morning with Simon, she thought dreamily. Another morning with Simon! And the cookies! Amanda burrowed further under the covers. Thinking of everything that could go wrong, she crossed her fingers and closed her eyes. Please let the cookies turn out all right.

Sleeping in a bed in a warm room seemed like the height of hedonism, and she hated to get up. But there was no use staying there. She had too much to do. With a quick movement of her hand, she flung the covers back and sat up, swinging her feet onto the floor. She plugged in her hair crimper before getting into the shower. Thank heaven for small favors. She could bathe and shampoo her hair in warm water in a warm bathroom. When she considered what original bathroom fixtures in a nineteenth-century inn would be like, she felt lucky the Canfields hadn't decided to "preserve" the original building. The last three days had been primitive enough.

She slipped into jeans, but this morning she decided on her pink angora sweater. Although it wasn't very practical to wear for baking, the color made her complexion glow. Maybe if she looked good enough, Simon wouldn't pay much attention to what the cookies looked like.

She carefully crimped the silver-blond strands. Humming to herself, she finished putting on her make-up and headed for the kitchen. Becki had called again last night, just before they'd gone to bed, promising the reinforcements would be on their way before dawn. So now all she had to do was wait.

"Good morning," Simon said as she walked in. "I was just about to see what was holding you up." He looked at her admiringly. "But one look and I can see that it was time well spent."

She smiled. "You don't look too bad yourself." Sleep had erased last night's fatigue lines from his face.

"Thanks. I've got breakfast ready. How does cocoa and toast sound?" He picked up the tea kettle. "I know you could do better, but there's something to be said for speed. This way, as soon as we get breakfast over with, we can start popping the corn."

Amanda glanced at the table which Simon had already set. "As a matter of fact, breakfasts"—*along with lunches and suppers*—"aren't my strong suit, so I'm glad you fixed it. Anything I can do to help?"

Simon grinned. "Just sit down and look beautiful while I serve you for a change." He returned to the stove for a stack of toast. "Your bread makes the best toast, Laura. That's another thing I'm really going to miss."

"Well, if you weren't going to a ski resort between Christmas and New Year's, I'd send some home with you. In fact, the next time I go into Salt Lake I'll air-express you some." She actually could bake good bread. She seldom did, however; there were just too many calories when she had the entire loaf to herself.

A cunning smile lit Simon's face as he slid into the chair across from her. "How often can I expect it?"

Amanda carefully cut a piece of toast in half. "How long do you think it'll take you to find a wife?"

"If I can count on regular shipments of bread, a long time."

Although he wasn't serious, Amanda felt flattered by his words. But she only said, "Start looking!" After they'd finished breakfast, she checked the cupboard for a pan to pop the corn in and discovered a long-handled wire popper.

"We're in luck!" she said, holding it up for Simon to see.

He looked puzzled. "You act as if you didn't know you had that."

"I didn't," she said, once again trying to think fast. "I thought Rob had thrown it out." She didn't elaborate on why Rob would have done such a thing.

"Well, I'm glad he didn't. It adds to the atmosphere."

Covering the bottom with popcorn, Amanda gave the popper to Simon. "Why don't you get started while I thread some needles."

They settled in front of the fireplace, a large bowl for the popped corn between them.

"I didn't realize they still made these," Simon said, giving the pan an extra shake.

"Unfortunately, like the stove and everything else from that era, they tend to burn things," Amanda said as she struggled to get the thread through the eye of the needle.

"Even so, there's something charming about shaking the popper yourself as opposed to watching the popcorn come out the spout."

The warm, comfortable feeling they'd shared last night spread between them, and she almost hated the thought that the others would arrive and shatter their rapport. If she were just Amanda Richards, even St. Thomas wouldn't offer as much as Spindrift Farm and Simon Kent. But she was Laura Reynolds.

Simon broke the spell. "For Christmas we always went to my grandparents' house. I liked that tradition—knowing they would wait until we got there to trim the tree, caroling the Sunday night before Christmas, opening a present each on Christmas Eve, waking up Christmas morning to find our stockings hung on our bedposts."

"What a wonderful memory." She shook her head. Appearances could certainly be deceiving. First she'd thought he was an old man, then a bachelor who enjoyed life in the fast lane, and now nearly every word he spoke confirmed his love of home life. "I think my favorite Christmas was the year we lived in Mexico City. I loved the piñatas, and the bright colors, and the candles in the windows. My parents took me to the cathedral for midnight mass on Christmas Eve, and I'll never forget the choir singing "Silent Night" in Spanish."

"None of your Christmases were the same?" Just the tone of his voice told her how foreign that type of childhood seemed to him.

"Not until Rob and I bought Spindrift Farm," she said, adding to herself, *If you don't count St. Thomas, that is.* But to reconcile her personal past with her pretend present, she said only, "Since we moved here we've developed our own traditions. But I like to try new things, too."

"So what are we doing new this year?"

"Making the tree decorations." To be absolutely truthful she should add "along with everything else," but she only said, "If you want, you can take some of them to use on your tree next year."

He gave her a cagey look. "Do I have to take the ones I make? I've never been too good at arts and crafts."

"You may pick the very best ones." Not that she thought he'd have that many to choose from. She was much better at assigning others to make decorations than actually making them herself. Even when her spirit was willing, her fingers didn't seem to be that nimble.

Simon tossed a kernel of corn into the air and caught it in his mouth.

"Can you do that again?" Amanda asked.

"Sure." And he did.

"Lucky."

So he did it again.

Amanda tried it and the popcorn arched over her head, landing somewhere on the floor behind her.

"No. Like this." He tossed up another piece and caught it.

She still couldn't see that he did anything special. Anyone should be able to do it. Trying to mimic him exactly, she tossed another piece in the air, and again it landed somewhere behind her.

Laughing, Simon moved the bowl and sat next to her. Picking up her wrist, he demonstrated how to flip it. This time the popcorn at least hit her face.

After about a dozen more fruitless efforts, Amanda grabbed a whole handful and tossed it all in the air at once. One piece finally hit her mouth.

He laughed. "Cheater!"

"Don't insult the hostess!" She took another handful and threw it at him. As if being attacked by popcorn were a call to arms, he launched a counterattack. A good half of what he threw went down the neck of her sweater. She grabbed a handful of popcorn and scrambled around behind him to dump it down his shirt. He twisted smoothly, eluding her, and she fell onto his lap. By this time, however, she was laughing too hard to roll off, and ended up sprawled across his legs. When he started to trickle more popcorn down her neck, she clutched his hand in an attempt to push it away. His eyes met hers and the deep blue sent a response through her that had nothing to do with being a good hostess or learning to catch popcorn in your mouth.

"What fun!" A voice spoke from the doorway. "I can see you've missed us."

Chapter 10

Letter from Spindrift Farm—

One of the best things about country living is just being yourself. There is no pretense, no putting on an act to impress the neighbors. Just simple honesty.

"Becki! Paul!"

Amanda rolled off Simon's lap and scrambled to her feet. Simon followed more slowly and with more aplomb. Becki, looking startled, stood just inside the door flanked by the two men.

Good grief! She'd forgotten her husband. "Rob! I'm glad you're finally here!"

The taller of the two men stepped forward, his brown eyes positively glistening with amusement. "Darling. Have you managed all right?" Before she knew it, she was in his arms, and he was kissing her. Thoroughly.

When he finally released her, she stepped back automatically, breathless with surprise. This actor certainly could work without a script! He kept her in the circle of his arms. He was perfect with his dark blond hair, thick mustache, and like Simon, a deep tan.

"Oh, Rob, I've missed you."

Hugging her against his side, he grinned again. "Not more than I've missed you, sweetheart."

"Simon, this is Paul Merritt, the photographer; Becki

Canfield, an editor from *Today's Home*; and, of course," she looked up adoringly into Rob's face, "my husband, Rob." Amanda turned to Simon. "And this is Simon Kent."

Although Paul had the build of a shaggy teddy bear, he had a cynical gleam in his eye as he extended his hand to Simon. The amenities stretched out as everyone said how glad they were to meet everyone else. Then Amanda looked meaningfully into Rob's eyes and swept her arm airily over the scattered popcorn. "I know how much you hate stringing popcorn, so Simon and I thought we'd do it before you got here."

Like the pro he was, Rob looked at Simon and shrugged his shoulders deprecatingly. "I like the way it looks when it's done, but stringing popcorn is not my idea of a good time."

Watching him pick up his cue line and carry it, Amanda had to admire his skill. But suddenly the charade changed. It had been bad enough when it was just she and Simon. Now here was another person pretending to be someone he wasn't, and two others acting as if they didn't know it was all a sham. This was even phonier, and she felt guiltier. Nothing about this week was real, except Simon. And it wasn't fair to use his life and his emotions to promote the magazine.

Simon, however, didn't seem to notice anything amiss. He held up his ten inches of strung popcorn for general display. "Then I'm sorry we didn't get more done."

Amanda could almost see the wheels turning in Becki's mind. Roughhousing with Simon on the floor wasn't on the program. She had to stay in character.

Amanda tucked her arm though Rob's and smiled up at him. "Will you cast your aversion aside and help us, now that we're committed. Besides, if you help, it'll go much faster."

"We can get some great shots of the three of you sitting in front of the fireplace with the popcorn in the middle," Paul said. "After we get settled in."

Amanda immediately remembered the problem of the bedrooms, but at least she'd discovered there was a hide-a-bed in the study. "Paul, I'm sure glad you were able to help us with this project. Becki said you've been having a little trouble with your knees, so I thought you'd rather use the study than a room upstairs. Here, let me show you where to put your things." She ushered Paul out into the hall and into the small side room before he could comment on her spur-of-the-moment fabrication.

Once out of earshot, she sighed heavily and smiled at him by way of apology. "Sorry about the knees."

"Actually," he said, dumping his camera bag and suitcase on the hide-a-bed. "My knees have been troubling me. This'll be fine."

Smiling to herself at the twists of fate, she pointed to the ceiling. "Unfortunately, the bathroom's through there. If you need anything, let me know and I'll try to help you out."

She left Paul to his unpacking, or washing up, or whatever he wanted to do, and hurried back to the others.

Becki and "Rob" had taken off their coats, and everyone was sitting, conversing politely. She heard Rob ask Simon about his months in captivity.

"Would anyone like a hot drink? We've got hot chocolate or hot chocolate," Amanda asked, knowing Becki was probably anxious to talk to her.

"Hot chocolate sounds heavenly," Becki replied immediately. "Let me help you."

Together the two women went into the kitchen.

"Well," Becki said, "how's it going?"

Amanda got out mugs. "As well as can be expected when you're living a lie." She spooned cocoa mix in each one while Becki filled them with hot water.

"I wouldn't worry about it, Amanda. After all, you are fulfilling Simon Kent's fantasy."

"The last couple of days have made me feel guilty that we're using him. Simon deserves better than to have his months as a captive used to promote *Today's Home*."

"You're doing it for him after all. And what does it really matter if he's with the real Laura Reynolds or if an article is written about him that generates more readers? The main point is that we're providing him the Christmas of his dreams. The publicity is only a by-product of this week."

"How do you think he's going to feel if he discovers this is all a sham?"

"How is he going to find out? Not from you. Not from me. And the others are being well paid to do their jobs."

"I'm not sure I can keep this up for another four days. Too often his expectations don't fit within my range of abilities."

"He thinks you're wonderful."

"He thinks Laura Reynolds is wonderful."

"You are Laura Reynolds to him, and so far Simon Kent seems to be having a marvelous time. Which means that you must be doing something right, in spite of your qualms." Becki smiled reassuringly.

With a shrug, Amanda accepted Becki's interpretation of what had happened. A denial wouldn't accomplish anything. She lifted the plate on the stove and stirred the coals inside. "I hate this range."

Becki laughed. "I keep trying to tell Ben it's carrying tradition a bit too far. But he maintains it saves on their heating bills, so who am I to complain?"

"If Simon hadn't known how to work it, we'd have been undone the first day."

"And you said nothing's gone right."

In the face of Becki's optimism, Amanda shook her head in resignation. Placing the mugs on a tray, she picked it up while Becki held the door open and they rejoined the others.

"Hot chocolate, help yourselves," Becki said. Obviously, she wasn't going to wait on anyone.

"This certainly hits the spot, darling," Rob said, after his first swallow. "Fantastic job!"

"It's hard to foul up cocoa mix and hot water," Amanda said dryly.

Becki winked at Amanda. "Laura can do anything."

"I can attest to that. She knew all kinds of ways to fix chicken while we were snowed in." Simon gave her a benevolent smile.

Becki looked astonished.

Putting down her cup, Amanda said, "Rob, why don't you come up with me while I show Becki her room."

When they got upstairs, Amanda pointed out the two vacant rooms.

"You mean I don't get to bunk with you, Laura?" Rob's eyes twinkled as he said the words.

"This fake marriage ends at the top of the stairs, and don't you forget it!" Amanda said sternly, although her eyes twinkled and she smiled to soften the words.

"Yes, ma'am." He saluted smartly before taking his bag into the bedroom. He stayed there only long enough to take off his coat before coming back.

"Anything else I need to be briefed on before I go downstairs? I've gone over the material Becki gave me."

"We don't have time to go into it now. While I'm sure that Simon would expect us to spend a few minutes together, he wouldn't expect us to be gone long enough to make you over into Rob Reynolds. Meet me in my room when we come up to bed tonight."

"And you said you wanted this marriage to end at the head of the stairs," he drawled, exuding a masculine charm that was undoubtedly his stock in trade.

"This is strictly business!" Amanda emphasized. "Now run down and play the genial host, and I'll be down in a few minutes."

A few minutes later when Amanda left her room, she met Becki coming out of her bedroom. "We better get back downstairs. I don't want to leave the rest of them alone for any length of time." She shook her head. "Does this remind you of an Agatha Christie mystery? All the guests are huddled together in an old house, afraid to leave the group because one of them is the murderer."

"We just have to make sure this week isn't the death of us," Becki added.

Simon had picked up the popcorn and had continued stringing it while he waited for the others to rejoin him. He had expected not to like Laura's husband, Rob, who appeared to be friendly, personable, and obviously in love with his wife. Perhaps his feelings hadn't been helped by finding Laura alone here, stranded for four days with no one to help her when the situation turned into an emergency. Of course neither Rob nor Laura could have anticipated the storm, and it was be unfair to hold the man's absence against him.

But there had been something else, too, and Simon couldn't quite put his finger on it. Maybe it was the uncertainty that crept into her eyes whenever Rob's name found its way into the conversation. Or the way she easily dismissed Rob's interest in their Christmas. However, the way Rob had greeted his wife left no room for doubt that they were still deeply in love, even after five years of marriage.

Rob interrupted his thoughts. "What are your plans for after Christmas?" he asked as he came into the room and settled himself comfortably on the couch.

Simon let his hands drop on his knees, the strung popcorn limp between them. "The bank's given me a month's leave, then I'm taking a permanent assignment in San Francisco."

Overhearing them, Paul Merritt called from the hallway, "San Francisco's a great city."

"I've only lived there on a temporary basis," Simon spoke up to include Paul in their conversation. "Almost from the beginning of my career, I've been traveling around the world, which is what I wanted to do when I went into international banking in the first place. Now I'm looking forward to staying put."

Paul entered the room. "I always wanted to be an AP stringer," he said. "See the world a little. Visit a war zone or something. Get some good credits."

"That sounds like a replay of my conversation with Laura."

Simon shot Amanda an amused glance as she sat down in the wing-back chair opposite him. "Doesn't anyone like hearth and home anymore? War zones leave a lot to be desired."

"Yeah, that's right. You spent a little time detained, didn't you?" Paul said, laying his camera on the lamp table and sitting down beside Rob.

"That's one way of putting it." Simon said ironically.

"How exactly did it happen?" Rob asked.

"We were taught preventive driving, but I became careless. Didn't use my driver for a few days and didn't change my route to work. The Shining Path, who hate everything connected with the U. S., captured me. It's risky to be an American in Quito, or for that matter, a Mormon missionary."

Wide-eyed, Becki asked, "Did they torture you?"

"Not as much physically as mentally. I was held alternately in a stockade and a hut, always aware that my captors were capricious and could kill me at anytime."

Everyone in the room became silent. Amanda was sure none of them had been that close to death, and all were shocked at Simon's experience. Finally, she said, "Anyone want a refill on the hot chocolate?" They all quietly nodded, so she gathered up the mugs and, carefully picking her way through the popcorn on the floor, made her way to the kitchen.

When Amanda returned, Becki was saying, "Why don't we string the popcorn while we drink our cocoa. Paul could take some pictures."

"It might be a good idea to clean up the mess first though, so everything will look neat and organized," Paul said. "We'd hate for anyone to get the idea the perfect Laura Reynolds is sloppy."

"Of course," Amanda agreed, going back in the kitchen for the broom. Feeling Simon's eyes watching her as he leaned against the doorway to watch her, she couldn't stem the flood of regret that washed over her. Already the arrival of the others seemed to diminish their relationship.

Paul positioned Rob on the couch with Amanda on the floor

at his knee. Simon sat a facing chair. They moved the coffee table back so the popcorn bowl sat prominently between them. When Paul started shooting, Amanda managed to turn her head slightly away from the camera.

Paul instructed them in an endless flow of talk. "Just talk, act natural, don't look at the camera. Laura, hold your string just a little to the left. Rob, tilt your head this way a little. Great. Great. Okay, one more."

All the spontaneity was gone, Amanda thought with an uneasy feeling. Simon looked suddenly remote. She wondered what people would see when they looked at this photograph.

"It's too bad you've already cut the tree," Paul said. "We could have gotten some good shots out in the woods."

"You're absolutely right, Paul," Becki said. "Why don't we re-enact it for the camera this afternoon?"

From her tone of voice, Amanda could tell that Becki was throwing herself wholeheartedly into making this week a success. Not that she would have expected any different from her.

"I think it's a great idea," Rob said, practically bounding to his feet. He spread his arms as if to encompass the whole outdoors and took a deep breath. "Fresh air, sunshine, exercise."

"Last year you hated it," Amanda reminded him emphatically.

"Last year, my dear, we had to slog through the mud." Rob pulled Amanda to her feet and into his arms. He nuzzled her neck and whispered, "Not too bad." She nodded and turned to the group.

"At least if this is going to be staged, we don't have to spend too much time trying to find the perfect tree." Her eyes met Simon's, but she didn't explain yesterday's adventure to the rest of them. "First of all," she added, thinking of the empty cupboards, "we need to unload the groceries from the car."

When Amanda saw the car, she wondered how they'd gotten all three of them into it. And from the looks of the boxes of food, Laura Reynolds was destined to spend lots of time in the kitchen over the next few days. Thinking of all the work ahead of her,

Amanda knew once again why she, personally, preferred spending Christmas in a hotel on a sunny beach.

Once everything was put away, Amanda went to her bedroom to get dressed. Although she'd feigned enthusiasm about Becky's idea, she dressed in her layers of outdoor clothing reluctantly. Already she'd had more than enough snow, and it seemed to her that an excursion out into the woods to fake cutting a tree could end disastrously. No matter how good an actor "Rob" was, he'd skated onto thin ice more than once, and their late night chat couldn't come too soon. If they weren't careful, all those little white lies she'd told Simon about their family would come home to roost.

And now she felt a stronger urgency than ever to keep Simon from discovering the truth. She didn't want him to feel deceived, and she didn't want him to despise her. If she failed in her portrayal of Laura Reynolds, one or the other or both of those possibilities would inevitably happen.

She'd better waylay Rob before the tree-cutting ceremony. With that in mind, she hurried as fast as she could. But when she knocked on his door, he didn't answer. Dandy! Maybe the others weren't downstairs yet. Dismay filled her when she found herself the last one to arrive in the living room.

"We waited for you, honey," Rob said, reaching out for her hand. She took it gratefully, thinking that even if they had a hundred hurdles yet to cross, he was doing his best to make the going as even as possible.

"The axe is hanging on a nail on the far wall of the utility porch," she told him. "Simon and I made sure we put it away."

With a wink, he took it along as they all went through the porch and out into the back meadow.

Trudging through the snow, in the path Simon and she had made yesterday, Amanda decided that there was a lot to be said for spur-of-the-moment activities. Although she acted happy and enthused, this calculated expedition lacked the life and excitement she'd felt just the day before with Simon. The snow was crunchier and the sky hazier, the wind brisker and the trees duller.

"This is great," Rob said, pulling on the branches of the nearest tree and sending a minor avalanche of snow tumbling over her. "You sure don't get experiences like this in Los Angeles."

"Los Angeles?" Simon asked, and Amanda stiffened. Ten minutes together and already they were flitting too near the flame.

"I grew up in Los Angeles," Rob said, undeterred.

"No kidding? I thought you'd always lived on a farm."

Rob looked at Amanda who tried to send him mental messages. It must have worked, because he pulled her into the circle of his arm and looked lovingly down into her face. "Nope. My interest in farming grew out of the first time I read *Mother Earth News,* and from meeting Laura. We bought Spindrift Farm when we got married."

Feeling as if a weight had been lifted off her shoulders, however temporarily, Amanda lifted her face, just in time to meet Rob's lips. She held the kiss no longer than necessary, then broke away.

"This looks like a good tree," Paul said. He walked around it once then stepped back to see its relationship with the other trees in the area. "Let's see. Simon, why don't you raise the axe as if you're chopping down the tree while Laura and Rob watch approvingly. Laura, stand here just to one side of Rob."

For nearly half an hour Paul placed them and shot, replaced them and shot again, moved to a different angle and shot again. Amanda made sure that no matter what the angle, a tree branch was in front of her face. By the time he said he'd had enough, Amanda thought her toes had frozen in her boots.

As the group returned to the house, Simon said, "Tell me more about the farm. What kinds of crops do you grow here?"

With "Rob" beside her, Amanda wasn't sure who he was asking so she quickly replied, "Actually, it's more of an enlarged hobby garden than a farm," she said. She doubted Rob would know unless he'd read the last two years worth of articles. "We have a small apple orchard and a big vegetable garden. We like to experiment with new strains of vegetables and berries, and we sell our produce at a roadside stand. But as you can see," she waved her arm around, "most of our farm is forest."

"The Caribou National Forest?" Simon asked slyly.

"Not quite," she said firmly. "We only have forty acres—not four thousand."

"And during the winter you write." This time Simon addressed Rob directly, and for the first time Amanda felt the actor was at a loss for words.

She took his arm. "I told Simon about your first western being published next year and how excited we are about it."

Before Rob could reply, Simon asked, "How did a city boy get interested in the Old West?"

"A matter of opposites attract, I guess. You know how it is. When you've never seen a live horse, reading about cowboys on the western frontier seems romantic." This time Rob seemed at ease. "So a western's the first thing I thought of writing."

Simon looked amused. "So much for writing about what you know. What's the story about?"

Without hesitation, Rob said, "A city-slicker lawyer who's trying to find a long, lost member of his family. On his way to California he ends up on a spread in Wyoming Territory smack dab in the middle of a range war."

It sounded like a pretty generic western to Amanda.

But as he talked, Rob's voice took on an exaggerated western twang.

"Are you using a pen name?" Simon asked.

Amanda wished that she'd never suggested Rob was a writer. Wouldn't it give everything away if Simon tried to find the book and couldn't? And even if that eventuality were ten or twelve months from now, she knew he wouldn't feel any less angry if he found out he'd been tricked.

"I haven't decided yet," Rob said. "What do you think about Jesse Franklin. Sort of a play on Frank and Jesse James."

"Too cute," Becki said.

"Then what about Nevada Jones?"

"Or Montana Smith." Amanda decided if he was going to turn it into a game, they might as well make it a good one.

"Or Joe Montana?" Simon proposed, his own voice rippling with laughter. "You could be a quarterback cowboy writer."

Seeing that they had sidestepped another danger zone, Amanda relaxed and listened to the others trying to outdo each other. With every suggestion, the ideas got more ridiculous. If she didn't know better, she'd think they were old friends, not total strangers.

Now that the groceries had arrived, Amanda had no excuse not to be Laura Reynolds at her best. She cooked pea pods and noodles along with braised sirloin tips, and then artistically arranged them on the plates. The peas circled the noodles and meat, making a wreathe on each one. Right out of Nonnie's column who, Amanda discovered, hadn't warned her readers that the gravy could be messy. But that was why paper towels had been invented, Becki told her cheerfully. She turned out to be no more adept at cooking on a wood range than Amanda was, but she did pitch in to help while the men talked.

Amanda didn't know what made her the most nervous—Rob on his own in the living room trying to answer Simon's questions or Rob in the kitchen where his unfamiliarity with the kitchen might be too obvious. At least Becki had visited the farm often enough to know her way around.

Keeping the uneven heat of the oven in mind, Amanda put together a Divine Decadence cake. To her chagrin, one side of it burned crisp, but it wasn't noticeable after she carefully drizzled chocolate icing over it. When she served it, she cut the pieces from the other side and surreptitiously tossed the burned side away.

After dinner she made wassail following the careful instructions from the column. Everyone except Paul joined in the decorating of the house, and Paul took pictures of everything, from every conceivable perspective, until he seemed part of the furniture. Amanda directed him not to worry about getting her in the pictures, since Simon was the important one.

Picking up a wreath of pine cones and holly, Rob opened the front door to hang it on the outside and began to sing, "Oh, by gosh, by golly, it's time for mistletoe and holly..."

Simon joined in and their voices melded into a marvelous duet of bass and baritone. Amanda knew her voice was thin, but it was true, so she picked up the melody line. Then Becki joined the singing.

When the song ended, Becki said, "This is good practice for when we go caroling."

"Caroling?" Amanda's voice was filled with apprehension. She'd hoped that Becki had forgotten about it.

"But, Laura, you always do that every year." Becki's tone was filled with amazement.

"Don't let me stop you. I'd love a chance to meet your neighbors and everything," said Simon.

Meeting their neighbors "and everything" was exactly what she was afraid of!

"Of course. We wouldn't want you to miss any of that," Amanda said, masking her fear with cheerfulness.

With those words Rob started singing, "It's beginning to look a lot like Christmas..."

And Amanda had to admit it did. The tree looked better than she had expected, what with the garlands of popcorn, the plaid bows, and the candy canes. Tomorrow they'd finish stringing the cranberries and make the ornaments.

With candles nestled among the greenery on the mantle, swags of pine branches decorated with plaid bows on the stair railings, lights in the windows, and her gaily painted ceramic creche from Mexico on the coffee table, the house really did have an enchanted look.

Rob dug sprigs of mistletoe out of the bottom of the last box and handed one to Simon. "Here you go. Put it wherever you want." Grabbing Amanda's hand, Rob made her hold a chair for him while he fastened his to the light hanging from the center of the room.

Simon hung his in the middle of the doorway. Turning to the others, he grinned and said, "I don't want to overdo the music, but..." He started singing, "Oh, ho, the mistletoe, hung where you can see. Somebody waits for you, kiss her once for me."

The words were hardly out of his mouth when Rob pulled Amanda into his arms and kissed her soundly. The shutter's clicking on Paul's camera reminded Amanda of her role, and she wound her arms around Rob's neck. The kiss lasted longer than she liked, and when Rob released her she was surprised to see Simon urging Becki under the sprig in the doorway. She found herself relieved that their kiss was merely perfunctory. Hoping to break up the kissing, Amanda said cheerfully, "Anyone ready for wassail?"

Chapter 11

Letter from Spindrift Farm—

> *The week before Christmas we join with family members to go caroling. This gives us a chance to sing the old carols, visit with our neighbors, and exchange gifts with them, sharing the spirit of the season.*

After an uneasy night, Amanda crept down the stairs well before she thought anyone else would be stirring. Laura Reynolds knew all sorts of tricks, had a repertoire of countless recipes, was a whiz in the kitchen, and could turn simple desserts into elegant gifts. Amanda Richards liked microwavable dishes straight out of the frozen-food case. She just had to get organized before anyone else came down.

Nonnie's prepared so much food, it shouldn't be much of a problem, Amanda thought gratefully. Still she shuddered at the thought of being on display.

Amanda had brought a box of hand-dipped chocolates, hoping that they would be enough. But Nonnie's column had featured home-made caramels, which Amanda felt obligated to produce. The recipe didn't seem to require precise timing, so she thought everything ought to go smoothly—at least more smoothly than with the candy canes!

What else? The cookies! It wasn't even 6:30 in the morning,

and Amanda felt as if her brain had gone on strike. She'd always liked to be in control, and right now she definitely wasn't. The tasks facing her seemed monumental. She needed luck and plenty of it. At least she and Rob had gone over the finer points of his biography. She prayed his conversation wouldn't be filled with potential bombs.

Tonight was caroling. She sighed. That meant taking small jars of mincemeat to the neighbors as gifts. Well, it looked as if accomplishing all this would keep everyone busy most of the day.

"Another morning, another meal! Need any help?" Simon said the moment he walked into the room.

"Just waiting for you to start the fire." Thank goodness, he'd arrived before Rob who undoubtedly had never worked a wood stove in his life.

Rob came in, followed closely by Becki. "Sweetheart, you jewel." He put his arm around her shoulder and let his thumb caress her cheek.

To Amanda's relief, Rob gave her a peck on the cheek instead of one of his full-tilt kisses. "Breakfast isn't quite ready, but it should be by the time Paul gets here."

Becki lowered her voice to a whisper. "I knew you could do it."

By skillful maneuvering, Amanda fried eggs and served pancakes without burning anything. After the dishes were washed, she sighed. One hurdle over and only a half dozen more to go.

Pasting a wide smile on her face, Amanda said, "We start with the caramels today."

"Want me to do the stirring or is this something that needs Laura Reynolds's sure touch?"

"Be my guest!" Amanda handed Simon the wooden spoon. "This is a fail-proof recipe."

His eyebrows rose a fraction. "Are you intimating that even I should be able to make them?"

"Exactly!" When they turned out perfectly, Amanda didn't know whether to be chagrined or relieved.

By noon, Amanda was exhausted and there was no relief in sight. "Next comes the bread," she announced, with forced enthusiasm.

Actually, mixing bread was one thing that she excelled at. She liked to make it, but when she did she found herself eating hot bread smothered with butter and jam by the loaf. So she seldom bothered.

Coming over to stand behind her, Simon said, "This brings back memories."

"I bet your grandmother made bread." Amanda casually tilted her face back to smile at him and found her head nearly resting on his shoulder. Her pulse quickened at his nearness and she self-consciously leaned forward to add more milk to the pan.

"How did you guess? Actually it was my mother. Store-bought bread was a treat when I was growing up. I never thought then that home-made bread would be a treat now."

Rob stepped between them. "Everyday's a treat when you're married to Laura," he said, giving her a hug. "We seldom buy bread."

"You're lucky all right." For a moment there was a twinge of longing in Simon's voice, but then he seemed to quickly recover and say dramatically, "If only you had a sister, Laura."

Keeping her eyes on the shortening, Amanda said, "I'd never consign my sister to living in the suburbs, an apron around her waist, children clinging to her skirts, with never a chance to go beyond the city limits!" However she wouldn't mind applying for the job herself.

"You've taught me a good lesson, Laura. Unless I'm interviewing at a home economics college, I'll know not to give away my expectations too soon!"

They nibbled on assorted cheeses and crackers for a quick lunch, then mixed and kneaded the bread doughs. Paul shot pictures from every angle, catching Amanda with flour on her face and Simon with an apron on.

While the bread was raising, Amanda reluctantly got out the

ingredients for the cookies. Stirring up the dough was simple, but cutting them out was another matter. First the dough was too thin and the cut-outs fell apart as she tried to slide them on the cookie sheet. Muttering under her breath, Amanda re-rolled the dough. This time it was thick enough, but it was so soft from the heat in the kitchen, that it stuck to the cookie cutters.

"Rob, dear, would you wash the cookie cutters for me?" she asked as she put the dough back in the refrigerator to chill again.

When she took out the other half, she found that even though the dough was the right thickness and the cookie cutters didn't stick, no one had explained how hard it was to get the cookies on the sheet in their original shape. The round balls were elliptical, the branches on the trees uneven, several toy soldiers were hatless, and only one Santa had both legs. And despite Amanda's careful watching, the first batch of cookies were burned black on one side of the pan.

Nothing like a good old wood range for uneven oven temperatures, she thought. She would have Nonnie include that in her next column to give a little touch of realism to that fairy-tale stuff she'd been writing!

But everyone seemed to be having a good time as they frosted over the mistakes with glee. She held her breath expecting someone to point out that the cookies bore no resemblance to those in *Today's Home.* At least her bread turned out like a picture in a cookbook.

Toward late afternoon, Amanda set out the jars of mincemeat, putting her own labels on them. She wouldn't have minded a nap, or at the very least, a break from the kitchen.

"After reading about last year's experiences caroling, I can hardly wait for tonight," Simon said with his unflagging enthusiasm. "And it'll be interesting to see your neighbors' reactions to getting Laura Reynolds's own homemade mincemeat."

"It's always fun," Amanda agreed. This wasn't exactly Laura Reynolds's homemade mincemeat, but the Silver Spoon's should run a close second. With any luck, she'd be able thrust it into their hands and be on her way before they had a chance to say "Thank you," let alone ask any questions.

She tied elaborate red and green bows on the mincemeat bottles with a sense of true satisfaction. When it came to creating art out of ribbon, she felt like a pro.

After supper they all bundled up for the out-of-doors again. Amanda shook with nervousness, although she didn't know if it was because of Simon's magnetic presence or her stark terror at being discovered for a fraud by her neighbors. Her hands trembled as she put on both pairs of long johns and two pairs of socks as a precaution against the cold.

Simon was so much fun, and despite her protestations to the contrary, she was beginning to believe that to be with him, she wouldn't mind a home in the suburbs. Maybe she wouldn't even mind white Christmases.

Shades of Brett! Simon wanted someone who could really cook, not just edit a magazine about it. That let her out unless she had a make-over, and she'd vowed never to do that.

Once again she was the last one down to the living room.

"I have special high-speed film, but most of the pictures will have to be taken with a flash," Paul told them. "So stay as close together as possible, and we'll get some great shots."

"With two beautiful women along, staying close won't be any hardship," Rob said, and this time he wrapped arms around both Becki and Amanda, guiding them in the direction of the door.

They started with the first house past the lane. It too was well away from the road, down a snow-covered drive, and sheltered by leafless trees. They piled out of the car and since Simon had the best sense of pitch, they let him begin the song. He started with "Winter Wonderland," and ended with "We Wish You a Merry Christmas." The people appeared at the windows, but to Amanda's relief no one came out.

After they finished singing, Amanda took the jar of mincemeat to the door and thrust it towards the woman who answered her knock. "Merry Christmas," she said. "We wish you a joyous holiday season."

As Amanda hurried back toward the rest of the group, the woman called a surprised, "Thank you."

Hearing the click of the door behind her, Amanda breathed a sigh of mixed excitement and relief. Everything had gone precisely according to plan. And in spite of the biting chill of the wind, the star-speckled sky seemed like a protective canopy, the sharp crackle of snow under their feet was a percussive accompaniment to their songs, and she couldn't imagine being anywhere else at that moment.

When she reached the others, she linked elbows with Rob and Simon, feeling a warmth creep through her body. "Isn't this great?" she asked. "I haven't had this much fun in a long time."

"Not since last year," Rob said mildly, squeezing her arm.

"Exactly," she agreed decisively. "The best time of the year at Spindrift Farm is Christmas."

"Hey, you guys," Paul called out. "Can we chit-chat later? It's too cold out here for conversation."

Amanda laughed and the trio quickly joined Becki and Paul at the car.

The next house they stopped at was closer to the road. They stood at the bottom of the steps leading to the front door and sang. When they finished, the whole family came out on the porch to thank them, and Amanda skipped up the steps and thrust the jar of mincemeat into the hand of the woman.

"Merry Christmas."

"And Merry Christmas to you, too." The woman held up the jar and read the label in the yellowish light on the porch. "Fresh mincemeat."

"Enjoy it," Amanda said and started to turn back down the stairs. Simon joined her, offering his hand to the man.

"From Spindrift Farm, Happy New Year."

"Sprindrift Farm?" the man said, his voice just curling into the lift of a question, and a lump came from nowhere to settle in Amanda's throat. Why couldn't Simon have kept the routine the same?

"Never heard of it," the woman said, bluntly.

"That's where Laura Reynolds lives," Simon said, "Have you read her magazine column?"

"I know everyone around here. Never heard of her."

Shaking her head, the woman turned to Amanda still looking puzzled.

Her heart pounding, Amanda said quickly, "I'm Laura Reynolds." Were they going to be found out at the second house! "And we're wishing you and all our neighbors the best Christmas ever. Best wishes for the coming new year."

She practically pushed Simon toward the steps, and the rest of the group quickly added their holiday greetings to hers, effectively eliminating any further chance for additional small talk.

Even when they were safely back in the car Amanda couldn't relax. That had been too close for comfort. Would the other neighbors have this reaction?

"It's too bad we don't have time to visit your neighbors, Laura," Becki said. "They seem like such nice people. But if we're going to deliver all these gifts we'll just have to keep moving."

"Besides, it's darn cold out there," Paul grumbled.

Amanda agreed. It suddenly seemed at least ten degrees colder than it had half an hour before.

As they lifted their voices in song at the third house a dog inside started to howl. They could hear the owners yelling at it to shut up, but the dog just got louder, joining them in song. A man opened the door and yelled out, "Will you get out of here, so I can get this dog quiet! Don't believe in this nonsense anyway." He slammed the door shut.

They looked at each other and burst into gales of laughter as they returned to the car. When they'd finally calmed down, Simon said, "I don't think he's a Laura Reynolds fan."

"He's new in town," Rob quickly spoke up. "Do you think the

dog is unfriendly or just showing his appreciation for good singing?"

At that the laughing started all over again. Amanda was grateful for one thing, Simon seemed to be having the time of his life.

Deep set from the road, the next place was a cottage-style house with what looked like a rose garden out front, buried under the snow. Before they were even finished with the first song, the front door of the house flew open and an elderly couple came out on the porch to listen. When the song ended, the man came down the steps to greet them.

"Merry Christmas," Amanda said, hoping to cut short anything he planned to say. "We brought you a little gift from Spindrift Farm to wish you happy holidays."

"This is mighty fine of you. My wife and I want you to come in and warm yourselves. We have some good eggnog and a fire. Come on in."

"We'd like to, but we have several more stops tonight." She thrust the mincemeat into his hands.

"You can spare a few minutes, and after that lovely song, we'd really like to get acquainted."

Amanda's heart pounded at the last word and she prayed Simon hadn't heard it.

"These folks are from a place called Spindrift Farm, mama."

"Spindrift Farm! Are you Laura Reynolds?" The woman sounded astounded, and she immediately grabbed Amanda's hand and began to pump it up and down. "Now, you really must come in."

Amanda entreated Rob with her eyes to get them out of the current mess, but before Rob could say anything, Simon was nudging her in the ribs. "We'd love to," he said, speaking for the group, and Amanda suppressed a groan. "It's really not that late, and it's always a pleasure to share a little Christmas warmth with neighbors."

Although Amanda shuddered at the challenge facing them, she meekly followed the elderly couple into the house. They were ushered into a small parlor, which looked as if it got used only when the minister came to visit on Sunday evening.

After making sure everyone was comfortable, the man settled his wife into a chair. "You just visit with these nice folks, and I'll get us all some eggnog."

"Laura Reynolds," the woman sighed. "What a pleasant surprise. You must be new around here."

Amanda could see a puzzled look gathering between Simon's eyes and wished again she hadn't been so eager for publicity.

The man spoke from the doorway. "So you live close?"

Avoiding his question, Amanda said, "Let me introduce you to Becki Canfield, an editor at *Today's Home*. Paul Merritt is a photographer who's staying with us. You know my husband Rob and this is Simon Kent."

"Becki Canfield." The woman mulled over the name for a few minutes, then smiled in recognition. "Are you related to our neighbor Ben? You don't look much like him."

"I think he's a distant cousin," Becki said, and Amanda hoped Becki never ran into this woman during some future visit.

"The mincemeat is fresh from Spindrift Farm," Amanda said, knowing that the longer they stayed in this house the heavier disaster hung over their heads. "We hope you like it."

"Well, of course we will. I've used your recipe time and time again. It has just the flavor we love. I can't wait to taste this made by Laura Reynolds herself. Do you mind?" She unscrewed the lid and picked up a spoon near her cup.

"What a nice thing for you to say." Amanda smiled graciously, and hoped to heaven the Silver Spoon's product remotely resembled the recipe Laura had included in her column.

Taking a big bite, the woman's face went from expectancy to disbelief. "What's in this?" she demanded.

Amanda was at a loss. What could she say? "Wh-what do you mean?"

"Well, you've got so much rum in it that the Women's Christian Temperance Union at the church would kick me out if they smelled my breath." She shook her head. "I'm sure you would want me to be honest."

Amanda wasn't at all sure of this.

"This isn't near as good. You should never have monkeyed around with your grandmother's recipe. Papa and I would never eat this with your original recipe around."

Before Amanda could say anything, the woman thrust the bottle back in her hands. She felt like a mother whose baby had just been called ugly. What did she do now?

Thankfully, the man returned carrying a loaded tray which he sat down on a low table near the woman's chair. The ritual of passing the drinks around kept conversation to a minimum. Amanda clung to the mincemeat, afraid to look at Simon and just wanting to be out of there.

Then Rob found the one topic that saved the day. "Are you planning to add any new roses to your garden this year?"

At the first opening Amanda nervously joined him in pursuing the topic. Anything to keep the subject off mincemeat or Spindrift Farm. All her knowledge had come from reading Nonnie's April column, but she was able to toss in a sentence here and there, hoping they sounded intelligent. By the time the cups were empty, they eagerly made their escape.

A cold wind had arisen, whipping down from the north, and it felt like heaven to Amanda's heated skin. She maneuvered herself next to Becki and a little away from the others.

"This isn't working!" she whispered urgently. "I can't stand this kind of stress."

"You did beautifully," Becki reassured her. "Don't worry."

"I think we're mad to continue with this farce."

Becki patted Amanda's arm in a gesture of comfort.

"Another time could be fatal." Somehow Amanda had to stop the caroling before visiting with neighbors, who didn't know her from Eve, collapsed their house of cards. *If I had the nerve*, she thought wryly, *I'd fake a fall. But could I make it look realistic?*

"Oh-h!" The next thing she knew she had skidded across a patch of ice and fallen against a pile of snow and ice that felt more like concrete. What was this? she thought in a mixture of embarrassment and discomfort. Wish fulfillment? She moved her legs, and pain radiated up her back. If she had planned her fall, she wouldn't have landed so hard.

Simon got to her first, though Rob was right behind him. Simon's hands closed around her arms as he hauled her to her feet. Brushing the snow away from her face, he asked, "Are you all right? What happened?"

"I just slipped. I'm okay." But her face felt skinned and raw, snow had filled her boots and gone down her neck, and her tail-bone throbbed up her entire back. But her mission had been accomplished. Surely no one would insist they go any further.

"We better quit for the night," Rob said. "Laura's coated with snow. It wouldn't be smart to let her get cold."

And without her to do the slave labor, everything would blow up in their faces, Amanda thought. "I'm already cold," she said, and as if to prove her point, her teeth began to chatter.

"So am I!" Paul said.

"And we already have more than enough shots of caroling." Amanda turned to Simon and placed her hand on his arm. "I'm sorry. It's been fun and I know you were enjoying it."

"Hey, that's all right. We can do the rest another night. Right now, you're the one we need to think about." He and Rob helped Amanda to the car and settled her comfortably in the middle of the front seat where the hot air from the heater could reach her quickly. Of course, they were only a couple of miles from the farm, so she doubted she'd catch much of a chill. But the melting snow was turning her already cold skin to ice.

When they arrived back at the farmhouse, Rob solicitously helped Amanda up the stairs. When they reached the privacy of her room, Rob grinned and said, "Quick thinking, Laura. That fake fall looked very real."

"It wasn't planned, or I wouldn't have landed so hard," she

151

said, rubbing her back. Despite the car's heater, she felt chilled to the bone.

"Let me run a hot bath for you. I bet I can even find Epson salts, which should ease your aches and pain." He disappeared into the bathroom. When he emerged, he said, "I was right, Epson salts tucked neatly under the sink."

"Thanks. See you downstairs in a little while."

"Why, Mrs. Reynolds," he drawled, "you trying to get rid of your husband?"

"Exactly." She grinned, pointing to the door. "Out!"

Sitting on the edge of the bed, she tugged off the numerous layers of clothing. By the time she went into the bathroom, the tub was nearly running over. Perfect, she could soak clear up to her neck.

When she got out, she slipped into a long, holly-red velveteen robe. It might not be Laura Reynolds's type, but it certainly was Amanda Richard's. She brushed her hair until it was a shimmering blond cloud. Between her fall and the bath, her face had a rosy glow.

As she descended the stairs, she heard Simon say, "The tradition and warmth of Spindrift Farm is fantastic. You and Laura have done a wonderful job giving this farmhouse such a hospitable feeling."

"I have to admit that most of it is due to Laura," Rob replied, glancing up toward Amanda. He stood and went to the staircase to meet her. "Feeling better, honey?" He placed his arm lovingly around her and guided her to the sofa where he sat beside her.

"Those Epson salts did the trick." She smiled at him. "I feel as good as new." If slightly shopworn.

Becki joined them, dropping into a deep easy chair. "Whew, it's been a long day." That certainly didn't sound like the ebullient Becki she knew, and Amanda gave her a sharp look.

"But great." Simon turned away from the fireplace. "Thank you for inviting me."

"We saw that spot on the news," Becki explained, "and

decided it would be good for the magazine."

Simon looked at Amanda questioningly. "That was your first consideration?"

"Well, at—" Becki said.

"No," Amanda protested. "After all you'd been through, we really wanted you to have a wonderful Christmas."

Simon moved to the chair facing Becki's and sat down. "So has it been worth it?"

"Better than we ever expected." Becki gave him a warm smile. "I've watched the shots Paul's taken, and I believe they'll be exactly what our editor had in mind. Laura's worried that we're not being fair to you. She doesn't want you to think we're using you."

"But you are, aren't you?"

Amanda interrupted. "In a sense. But we're trying to give you what you wanted at the same time. Are we doing that?"

He leaned back and stretched his legs in front of him. The fluttering shadows from the fire softened his strong features. "I'd say so. It's been a great week so far. One I'll remember for a long time to come."

Becki nodded with satisfaction. "Good, and since people will want to read about your perfect week, it should increase our circulation."

Amanda could have strangled Becki at that moment. Did she have to keep on about the circulation?

Simon glanced towards Amanda and she shrugged, giving him a noncommittal look. She hoped he got the message that she didn't really care whether or not they got the additional readers, she just wanted him to have a memorable time. And somehow in the last four days, that's all she'd come to care about.

Chapter 12

Letter from Spindrift Farm—

> *Two of my favorite childhood memories are making angels
> in the snow and playing fox and geese—my heart hammer-
> ing like crazy as I ran from the fox along the slick path we
> had trampled in the snow.*

Slowly filtering into her consciousness, Amanda noticed the
smell of bacon. It laced the air around her, nudging her awake.
Rolling onto her back, she opened her eyes and savored the heavenly aroma. She didn't even have to think what to fix. Someone
else had beat her to it.

She threw off the covers and gingerly swung her legs over the
side of the bed, wincing at the stiffness of her muscles. Despite
the hot bath, the fall had jarred her enough that she was stiff and
sore this morning. But she felt good. Somehow she'd survived
cooking during the day and caroling at the neighbors' during the
evening.

After a quick shower, she dressed in her yellow sweat suit. The
softness of the fleece added to her feeling of well-being. She
fluffed up her hair so that it tumbled becomingly around her
face. After careful use of her make-up brushes, she felt ready to
face whatever the day brought.

In the kitchen Simon presided over the stove, a spatula in one hand as he monitored a griddle of pancakes. Paul and Rob sat at the table, and Becki was mixing orange juice at the sink.

"Good morning, sweetheart," Rob said, leaving the table to greet her with a kiss when she entered the room. "Do you mind that I let you sleep in?"

"Good heavens, no! Not when this is what I get when I'm sleeping. Good morning, everyone."

"Are you all right today?" Simon asked, his voice filled with concern. "No ill effects from your fall in the snow?"

"Other than being a little stiff from muscles I haven't used since my last mishap, I'm fine."

Amanda took two of the large fluffy pancakes. Simon was a much better cook than she was although, of course, she planned on keeping that little secret from him. Liberally buttering her pancakes, Amanda poured maple syrup on them and took her first bite. "Fantastic! Just as delicious as they look. You certainly don't need a wife like Laura Reynolds. You have all the attributes yourself."

His smile showed sincere pleasure. "Coming from you that's a real compliment."

"What's on the agenda for today?" Paul asked. "I hope you've planned something for inside. I'm tired of frostbite."

"Don't tell me you're afraid of a little weather? This from someone who wants to be an AP stringer?" Amanda teased.

"But *Today's Home* isn't the AP," he replied, "and I prefer heat."

"A man after my own heart," Amanda said, giving him a teasing smile. The other three looked at her as if she'd lost her mind, and she quickly remembered the role she was playing. For the first time she appreciated how hard it must be for actresses to stay in character when they were filming a movie in bits and pieces.

"You all know how I like the sun. Just because I love Christmas in Idaho doesn't mean I can't like the sun." The last words were said firmly, in a tone brooking no arguments.

Simon, who had started taking dishes from the table, turned

to Amanda, "So what are we going to do today? Inside or out, it doesn't matter to me."

"We need to make the ornaments for the tree. Then we can finish decorating it." She gave a silent sigh of relief, but at the same time couldn't resist a feeling of satisfaction because the house did look like something out of *Today's Home*. Wonderful. In fact, a house like this was just what she had in mind when she'd planned the December issue.

"That should take most of the morning. What do you think about going on a picnic this afternoon?" She looked around the room expectantly, wondering if Paul would resist the idea.

"In the snow?" Rob's tone indicated he couldn't believe what he was hearing. "Never heard of such a thing."

Shooting him a quelling look, Amanda said, "Don't be funny. We do it every year!"

What was going on here? At first Simon had thought something was wrong about Laura, but now he wondered about Rob. He said cautiously, "I haven't been on one since I was a kid. But the way you described it in your column sounded like fun."

Rob and Paul both looked at him uncertainly, as if time spent away from the fire was beyond the call of duty.

Then Rob's expression changed to one of teasing indulgence. "I just like to give Laura a bad time. I especially like to warm her up when we come home."

Amanda forced herself to look at Rob as if she got the greatest of pleasure from that little exercise herself. "We're all agreed then?"

She noted that although everyone nodded their heads, it was with differing levels of enthusiasm. "I'll get the materials for the ornaments, and we can make them on the dining room table."

"Let me give you a hand," Simon said, following Amanda out onto the porch.

"These two cartons contain everything we need," she said pointing to a couple of boxes she'd stacked next to the wood.

"If this is all fabric, I can see we may be busy sewing all day."

"No law says we have to use every scrap." She lifted the top box which was the smallest and left the other one for Simon. "The stuffing is what takes up most of the space."

He hefted the other box, and they rejoined the others. "Don't forget you promised me some of these ornaments. And I get the ones made by you."

She flashed him a quick grin. "Right you are—if you want them." She left a question in her voice. If by any remote chance his mother had made ornaments, Simon was undoubtedly more adept at this than she was. Amanda pinned the pattern to the felt and began cutting.

Rob had the romantic good-looks of a soap opera hero, and while he was certainly warm and friendly enough, he didn't attract her. On the other hand, Simon certainly did. The mischievousness in his eyes and the quirk when he smiled made her pulse race. Looking up from the patterns, she studied Simon's mouth as he intently put the pieces together. Firm, but softening when he was amused. She wondered what it would feel like on hers in a deep, soul-satisfying kiss. Her breath caught. She shook her head. Forget it. If that happened, there went her life.

Paul stood at the end of the table shooting pictures. With all the film he was using, the magazine wouldn't show a profit for months.

"Give your shutter a rest, Paul, and come with me. I need to run some errands," Becki said decisively. And off they went.

It took Simon and Amanda nearly two hours to finish the ornaments. She'd never realized how important getting just the right amount of glue was. Some ornaments refused to stick together, and others were so soaked they looked as if they'd never dry. By the time they finished, she was sick of the entire project, but Simon looked pleased with the result. Any other man would have seemed less masculine to be so enthused about making cookies and ornaments. However, Simon exuded so much self-confidence that his masculinity was only heightened by his enthusiasm.

Glancing at her watch, Amanda said, "I think I'd better get the roast on for supper and fix lunch." Her jobs never ended. In her next columns, Nonnie needed to tone down all the activities. No one could keep up the schedule of wonderful Laura Reynolds without dropping from exhaustion.

Rob followed her into the kitchen. "Do you know where Becki went?" When Amanda shook her head, he said, "Over to Johnsons' to see about using their sleigh on Christmas Eve. I think we're about to fail our next test. I've never been around horses in my life, and Becki informed me that I'm expected to hitch Old Dobbin to the sleigh and get us to the church on time."

"Let's just pray they won't loan it to her. At this point what else can we do?" She started scraping the carrots. Why couldn't Becki just leave well enough alone?

Before Rob could say anything else, Simon came in with his coat on. "I noticed that the woodpile is getting a little low. Would you like some help in chopping some more?" he asked Rob.

Rob looked as if he'd just as soon be chopping snakes.

He asked warily, "Do you know how to handle an axe?"

"Yes. I had plenty of practice as a kid. We always went up in the hills each fall and brought down a pickup load for our fireplace. I think I can remember the basics once I get started."

"Living here has given me a respect for the type of labor that built this country."

Simon laughed. "Twenty-five years ago was hardly pioneer times. But I know what you mean."

"Let me grab my coat." A minute later he rejoined them and the two went outside. Amanda peeked out the window. Simon was swinging the axe, and Rob was stacking the wood.

Amanda picked up the paring knife and started peeling the potatoes. Cooking on this stove gave her a new appreciation for modern conveniences. One thing for sure, from now on she would line out any mention of the virtues of a wood range in Nonnie's column.

They finished decorating the tree before lunch. Amanda had to admit that old-fashioned trees were charming. This one looked spectacular; in fact, the whole house did. After they were snowed in she'd doubted they'd be able to pull it off.

Simon was strangely silent. She didn't feel like saying much herself. There were only forty-eight hours left before Simon disappeared. Would she ever have a chance to straighten all this out? Or would he just vanish from her life completely? Was he even interested in her? Maybe she was blowing her feelings way out of proportion. Would she find Simon this attractive if she hadn't been caught in a snowstorm with him? Her heart gave a resounding "yes."

She wrestled with the problem while she fixed a myriad of goodies for today's picnic and tomorrow's midnight supper. Then she started on some of the food for Christmas dinner.

How could she tell Simon she wasn't really Laura Reynolds? Especially after all Becki's comments about getting more subscribers. Taking advantage of Simon for publicity now seemed so tawdry. She'd gone too far this time in thinking up new ideas for the magazine.

Amanda sighed. No one had offered to help with the food, and she was feeling more and more put upon. Then they all trooped back into the kitchen—with smiles on their faces as if they hadn't a care in the world. Becki's role was just to be cute and charming. Rob had an easy secure job as a happily married husband. Simon only had to be a guest. And what was the world coming to? Paul even looked happy. Right now she felt as disgruntled as he usually looked.

"What heavenly smells," Becki had the nerve to say. "Neal Johnson is going to bring his horse and sleigh over about three so we can get pictures of you with the sleigh, getting ready to go to the community church services. Then if the ones we take of the actual trip don't turn out, we'll have some."

Smothering a groan, Amanda said, "We'll need to leave right away for our picnic."

"Where did you have in mind to go?" Rob asked, plainly not enthused that this was still on the agenda.

Amanda looked amazed, as if she couldn't believe he would ask such a stupid question. "To the pond where we always picnic. Is there someplace else you'd rather go?"

That last statement must have been sheer inspiration. But Amanda knew that if he led the group anywhere, they'd probably be lost for the winter.

"No, I just wondered if you had a better idea," Rob said hastily.

"Now I ask you, could anyone improve on Laura's ideas?" Becki said with a Cheshire smile that Amanda was sure didn't fool anyone.

"Becki, I need to go over our plans with you," Amanda said, wondering what else her assistant might spring on her.

"Can it wait awhile? I need to get the snowshoes out."

"Snowshoes?" Rob and Amanda chorused.

"Yes. Snowshoes. Since you two go snowshoeing every winter I thought it would be fun to give Simon a chance to try it."

Amanda and Rob looked at each other. This time in perfect sync. What else could Becki possibly dream up? Well, she for one wasn't going to pretend she could snowshoe. She couldn't. The closest she'd ever come to snowshoeing was reading Nonnie's column on it. What luck that the Canfields snowshoed.

"Becki..." she started.

Just then Simon said, with his old enthusiasm, "That sounds like fun."

"I suppose you snowshoed all over Montana when you were a boy?" Amanda couldn't keep the hostility out of her voice.

"No," he said, matter-of-factly, shaking his hands dry. "I've never tried it. Why don't I go with Becki to get them?"

"Becki, before we leave this house for any picnic, I want to talk to you."

But it didn't turn out that way. When Simon and Becki came in, they were laughing over Simon's first experience on snowshoes. Amanda felt like Cinderella watching her stepsister having a good time with the prince. And Becki stuck to the prince, never giving Amanda a chance to talk to her.

Snowshoeing turned out to be nearly impossible. She tipped over forwards several times just trying to get started. "You're as inept as I am. Is it possible you overstated your expertise a little in your book?" Simon said, his eyes twinkling.

"Snowshoeing isn't something you never forget, like riding a bike," she only said.

Finally, she got the knack of it, but in order to keep her balance, she could only move at a snail's pace. Simon seemed to be a natural athlete. He clumped along easily with no problem, keeping Rob and Amanda company. Becki plowed ahead, effortlessly pulling the sled which carried the food and some wood. And Paul brought up the rear, getting shots of their efforts.

The going wasn't easy, and after what seemed like hours, no one could convince her that the pond was only a mile away. Maybe as the crows flew in the summer, but in the winter on snowshoes, up and down hills, it seemed at least ten.

Finally they came upon a sheltered gully where two felled trees peeked out from the snow. Removing their snowshoes, the entire group busied themselves. Rob and Simon built a fire. Tired beyond belief, Amanda forced herself to the sled. She'd packed the food in thermal containers, and it was hot. They roasted wieners, which Amanda smothered with chili, and they drank hot cider. For dessert they had blueberry cobbler.

Everyone exclaimed over the food, and Paul took picture after picture. At this point, Amanda didn't care whether she was in them or not, she just wanted to rest.

Looking at the snow-swept meadow next to the frozen pond, Simon said, "How about a game of Fox and Geese."

Amanda's tiredness vanished at the warmth in his voice. "Another childhood favorite, I'll bet!"

"How did you guess?"

"Prescience."

Becki looked eager, and she motioned Paul to join them.

"We'll follow while you break the trail," Rob said.

Laughing, they tramped out the largest Fox and Geese circle Amanda had ever seen. She wasn't particularly good at estimating distance, but she thought the spokes running out from the center must be at least forty feet long.

"Simon's it!" Amanda yelled, and they all ran. She tore down one of the paths. Simon waited where he was until she reached the circle, then he ran after her. When she started running, the adrenaline started flowing, and all of a sudden it was as if she were really running for her life. Squealing her plight, she ran from him, all the while trying to both watch where she was going and monitor his progress behind her. In the periphery of her vision, she saw him gaining on her.

In a final burst of speed, Amanda tripped over her own feet. Because he was so close, she effectively tripped Simon also. Laughing, she rolled over to look at him, her face wet with snow and her hair tumbling free of her cap.

Poised just above her, Simon's face was only inches from hers. His eyes were dark and shining with laughter, his expression free and open. In the days since his arrival he'd lost the last of his haggard, captive look, and suddenly, Amanda's heart was pounding raggedly in her chest. And not from running.

She wanted him to kiss her. She wanted his lips to lower slowly to hers and his hands to find their way into her hair. She wanted him to wrap her so close against him that their hearts would beat as one.

And as if he could read her mind, his hands found their way into her hair, and his lips lowered slowly to hers. Then abruptly he stiffened and lifted his head before rolling away. "What the hell am I doing?" He reached down and pulled her up. "Forgive me. I've been in the jungle too long."

"What are you two doing? He tagged you fair and square, Laura. You're it." Rob called from across the circle. Becki and Paul stood watching from the center.

Chapter 13

Letter from Spindrift Farm—

The Christmas Eve service at the village church is the cul-mination of all our preparations. We go in an old-fashioned sleigh. On the way, wrapped in blankets to shield us from the chilly temperatures, we sing carols. On the return home our voices are stilled as we savor the beauty of the night and con-template the Christmas message, "Peace on earth, goodwill toward men."

Amanda was grateful the picnic was over. On the way home, Simon was as silent as she was. What else could she expect? He was an honorable man. And what did a well-known, happily-married woman say to a man she was falling in love with? Falling in love with? Forced closeness might make it seem like love. But in five days? Only in the movies! Besides, she didn't really know how Simon felt. While he might be relieved to find out she was single, he might, on the other hand, be justifiably angry and unforgiving at the wholesale deceit they'd practiced. He certainly deserved more than to be used.

But did he feel anything for her? For all his talk about want-ing to get married and settle down, a man still didn't wait until his thirties to think about marriage without some pretty solid reasons holding him back. It might be the "nineties," but in this particular situation she couldn't risk taking the lead in revealing her feelings.

Amanda had always considered herself fearless, but right now she didn't feel so brave. As she pulled her sweater off, she noticed her hands trembled. Taking a deep breath, she made her decision. Regardless of the consequences, she would tell him.

When the sleigh arrived at the farm, Simon sought the privacy of his room eagerly where he took his time changing out of his wet clothes. How the hell had he let it happen? What a stupid kid's game! Obviously he should have picked one of the others to chase, and yet she had been the closest. He'd never imagined it would end with her tantalizing green eyes looking into his.

So what should he do? Thank these wonderful people and leave, today? Disappoint them in all the preparations they'd made to provide him with the Christmas he'd wanted? Or stay, and stay as far as possible from Laura?

Why couldn't Rob have been old and garrulous, making life difficult for everyone around him? Why did he have to be funny and young, someone with all the qualities of a good friend? Why couldn't Laura have been middle-aged and matronly? Why couldn't she have been crotchety and bossy, a wonderful cook but a horror to be around? But she was none of those things. Instead she was young and beautiful, competent but vulnerable, full of life, but serious too.

And why did he have to fall in love with her?

How had he missed the danger signs? Or maybe there hadn't been any. Except every time they'd started to say the same thing at the same time, he should have seen it coming. Every time their hands had touched while baking in the kitchen, he should have felt it.

He didn't feel much better when he was dressed in dry clothes. Downstairs the fire had died down so he threw another log on it. Tomorrow would be Christmas Eve, and the next day he could legitimately say good-bye.

This week had been balm to his soul and in some ways he felt healed from his ordeal. At peace. Thanks to the hospitality of Rob and Laura. Laura might look like a cover-girl, but when it came right down to it, she was as old-fashioned as her column. He'd always admire the honesty with which the two lived their lives. He only wished he could have found Laura first.

Amanda took great pains with her make-up and hair, and then slipped into red velvet pants and a heavy gold sweater with a glittery Christmas tree on it. But the horse and sleigh arrived before she had a chance to get Simon alone.

She joined Rob and Simon in front of the house. Despite the bright sun, the temperature was well below freezing and her facial muscles felt frozen, so much so that she could manage only one expression. Paul kept trying to get her to talk and smile, do something else, but she simply couldn't. Her face refused to respond.

Finally when Paul had them seated just the way he wanted and when Amanda had managed to pull her muscles into a less grim expression, she saw a car turn into the lane. She watched uncomprehendingly as it bounced over the ruts in the drive, nearly skidding to a stop in front of them. Then as the insignia on the side of the car finally registered, her heart skipped a beat. Oh, no! The sheriff! Just when she'd had hope everything would work out. She crossed her fingers.

As the two men climbed out of the car, Amanda recognized one—the forest ranger. What was he doing here? She knew for a fact that the front lawn wasn't Caribou National Forest. She glanced at the other man as he crossed the few feet to the sleigh. A uniformed policeman.

"Ben around?" the policemen asked.

Becki spoke up. "He's in the city. I'm his sister Becki. Is there a problem?" She spoke decisively as if to challenge their presence on the farm. This was a side of Becki Amanda had never seen before

"Those are the two, sheriff." The ranger pointed at Amanda and Simon. "They claimed this was Spindrift Farm. I wasn't convinced then, and after discussing it with my wife, we realized that the place they claimed was Spindrift Farm was actually Ben Canfield's."

Now not only Amanda's face but her heart seemed frozen and she could only take ragged shallow breaths, not from the freezing temperature, but from terror. She glanced at Simon. He stared at the two strangers, his face impassive. She had wanted to tell him the truth, but not this way. Hot tears drained down her throat. He'd never forgive her.

"Gentlemen, the explanation is simple, but let's go up to the house where we can be warm and where we won't interrupt the shooting of pictures for *People Magazine*." Becki started to lead the men away.

"No, stay here. I think this is something I want to hear," Simon spoke decisively, and with a quick movement he jumped down from the sleigh. Amanda, followed by Rob, joined the circle.

"This is Simon Kent." Amanda motioned towards Simon. "You probably saw him on TV. He just returned a week ago from being held captive by a group of rebels in South America."

"That's not what this is about," Simon said impatiently, his eyes narrowing as he looked at Amanda. "Whose farm is this?"

"My brother Ben's." Becki spoke quietly without her usual enthusiasm.

"Then who are you?" He looked at Rob.

"Mark Shafer."

Simon turned to Amanda. "No wonder you don't look like the picture on the cover of the book. You aren't Laura Reynolds."

"No, I'm not." Amanda could barely speak past the lump in her throat. "This isn't the way it looks. After the ordeal you'd been through, we wanted you to have the Christmas you'd dreamed about." She waved her hand towards the house. "This was all for you."

"Is it? I have it on good authority," he said, giving Becki a quelling glance, "that this is about increased circulation. But the charade is over. You don't have to pretend another minute. Just as soon as I can get my bags packed, I'm out of here." He stalked toward the house without a backward glance.

"That still doesn't answer our questions, ma'am. What are you doing here?"

"I'm Ben's sister," Becki said heatedly. "He gave me the use of his house for a Christmas story, but thanks to you two, everything is ruined. Come on, I'll call Ben, and he can explain it." Becki started toward the house, the two officers following.

Amanda stared at the retreating figures and her chest tightened. She shook her head in disbelief at how quickly all her hopes and dreams had collapsed. She was a fool to believe anything could ever have worked out between Simon and herself. She'd known from the beginning that he'd react this way to the truth.

The pain came in waves. Each one more intense until they encased her heart. Her eyes filled with tears, and only through sheer willpower was she able to hold back the sobs. How could she have been so stupid?

"If you're interested in Simon, you'd better catch him before he leaves." Rob's voice broke the silence.

Her body seemed congealed by pain, making words impossible. She had only herself to blame. But Simon had always been reasonable, surely he'd at least listen to her explanation. Rob was right, she had to catch him.

Amanda raced to the house. Once inside she ignored Becki and the two men and ran up the stairs to Simon's room. The door was open and without knocking, she entered. He was grabbing clothes out of drawers and slamming them into his suitcases without any regard for neatness and order.

"Simon—," she said hesitantly.

"What do you want?" he demanded, not looking up.

"A chance to talk to you."

"What about? *Today's Home* saw an easy way to build circulation and used me." Still without looking at her, he turned to the closet and yanked out several shirts. "There's nothing more to say. So go."

"You owe me a chance to explain," she pleaded.

At this he looked up, his blue eyes blazing. "I don't owe you anything. After posing for hundreds of pictures and an article in *People,* I've more than paid for my five days here."

Amanda closed the door and leaned against it, wondering how the pain could be so intense and at the same time numbing. She fought the tears, not wanting him to see how hurt she was. "I saw you on TV. I found what you said interesting, and I thought it would be perfect. You'd have a wonderful holiday and *Today's Home* would have marvelous publicity. Laura is just like her column—warm. I knew she'd love to have you. But at the last moment she couldn't and..."

"And not wanting to see a chance for publicity to slip away, you quickly filled in," he said scathingly.

She ignored his words. "Laura herself suggested the whole plan."

"Of course," he said, obviously not believing her.

"At first I felt we were taking advantage of an old man," she scowled at him, "which by the way you aren't. But believing that we could at least give you a wonderful experience, I decided to do it."

"Just exactly what I said. You'd do anything for your magazine." He took the last two sweaters from the closet, slammed the door shut and stuffed them in the suitcase.

"I'm sorry. I never—"

"Sorry you were found out," he said harshly. "For two cents I'd expose your scheme, but you're not worth it." He slammed the lid shut on his cases and snapped the locks. Picking them up, he came towards Amanda until their bodies were nearly touching.

Tentatively, she laid her hand on his sleeve. "Simon—"

He shrugged her arm off. "There's nothing else to say. It's perfectly clear. Anything for a few new readers, including making a sap of the guy who can make it all happen for you. Is your job so important to you that you would do anything, commit any deceit, play with someone's life? Has there been anything honest about this entire week?"

Not giving her a chance to reply, he continued, "I never dreamed you could be lying. You've got that innocent act down pat. After four days of being stranded alone together, I thought I knew you. But, lady, I don't even know who you are." He smiled bitterly. "Not that I care." Reaching for the knob, he wrenched the door open.

Amanda watched his back as he headed down the stairs. She'd known from the beginning that this was never going to work. Why had she let herself be caught up in it? She should have stood up to her granddad, but that wasn't the way she'd been raised. Pain gripped her. The one thing she hadn't known was how much it would hurt. Why couldn't Simon Kent have been an old man? Why did it have to hurt so much?

Slowly, Amanda followed him down the stairs and watched silently as he grabbed his coat from the closet, shrugged into it, and without a word headed for his car.

Never glancing at the house as he turned the car around, Simon left.

The officers were apologizing as they came into the living room with Becki.

"Oh, it's nothing, you've just cost us thousands of dollars." Becki ushered them out. Sighing, she turned to Amanda. "The only bright spot in this fiasco, is that we have some good shots for *People*.

"We can't." Tears stung the corners of Amanda's eyes. "We've done enough. I'm sorry, but I can't stay here another minute." Sapped of her energy by all the events of the day, she wearily returned to her room and changed into something less glittery before throwing her clothes and personal items into the cases with the same speed and abandon as Simon had.

Going downstairs, she hunted up Rob and Paul. "Do either of you know how to get a car out of the ditch?"

"I think a little weight on the rear end should do it," said Paul, for once not disagreeable over going out in the cold.

"Yeah, if we both push on it, we ought to be able to get it free," Rob added.

Slipping on her coat and gloves with the others, they went out to the car. It only took a few minutes and the car was in front of the house with the motor running to warm it up.

Through a mist of tears, Amanda packed her nativity scenes. Thinking of the day she and Simon had put them out and how much she had wanted him to kiss her. She looked around the house at all their handiwork and she couldn't resist taking a few of the candy canes and a couple of the felt ornaments. Then, her chest still in knots from the pain of Simon's words, she was off. Off to the city. She'd had enough of Spindrift Farm, real or imagined, to last her a lifetime.

Chapter 14

Letter from Spindrift Farm—

A new year has started here at Spindrift Farm. The meadows and the woods are blanketed with snow. Everything is serene and peaceful as we gaze across our land, contemplating the fruition of our plans.

Simon ducked his head down and hunched his shoulders in an effort to protect himself against the fierceness of the wind. The cavernous streets of San Francisco seemed to give impetus to the wind's momentum. If he didn't know better, he'd almost believe he was back in Montana where there was nothing to stop the wind as it howled across the northern plains.

Br-r-r, he couldn't wait to get inside the bank. He never thought he'd say it, but right now the jungle seemed almost good to him. Only two and a half more months of this weather and spring should be here. If he lived that long. The month since he'd left Spindrift Farm, make that Ben Canfield's farm, had seemed a lifetime. He'd thought the anger he'd felt towards *Today's Home* staff—*make that the fake Laura Reynolds*, he said to himself—would dissipate. But it hadn't.

While he was held captive, he'd resolved never to get upset over trivial matters again. And anything short of life and death was a trivial matter in his book. However, he couldn't shake his feelings of hostility towards Laura. How could she have deceived him that way?

Simon quickened his pace. He'd thought the woman was perfect; in fact, he'd been close to falling in love with her. He had agonized over being honorable, and then to find out she wasn't even married!

My first instincts told me there was something wrong, he berated himself. *I should have followed those instincts.* How could he have missed the clues—cutting a tree on federal land, visiting with neighbors who were obviously strangers, not knowing about the kerosene lamps or the radio? He'd been blind to everything but her blond beauty and her seeming sincerity. But how could he have done anything other than what he'd done, with a blizzard raging? He didn't know.

Simon checked his watch, seeing that he was nearly late for his first appointment. He pushed through the glass doors of the First Federal Building and hurried through the crowd to the elevators, barely making it in time. He hoped this wasn't indicative of what his entire day was going to be like.

Going out to his secretary's desk a couple of hours later, his heart gave a quick leap when he saw Laura Reynolds, or whoever she was, entering the office. What was she doing in San Francisco? The strap of a large brown shopping bag hung over one wrist. Maybe she'd come to shop and had run out of money. But she was in the wrong department if she needed a loan.

Her face was rosy and she looked windblown, but—he had to admit—gorgeous. Beauty wasn't enough, however; he knew how ruthless she could be in order to succeed. Everything else she'd said could be a lie. He knew nothing for sure about her, and steeling his heart, he said sharply, "Yes?"

"I promised you some bread. I'm just delivering." She held the bag out to him.

Simon looked skeptical, then peered out into the hall and behind the file cabinets. "Don't tell me you're after more publicity?" Then anger surged through his body. "Is Paul hiding around here somewhere taking pictures of your largess?"

"No," she said with asperity. "Bread is the symbol of hearth and home. I just wanted to wish you well in your new home."

"You came eight hundred miles to deliver bread? I don't believe it. What are you really doing? Trying to soften me up, so I won't go public with the truth about a week with Laura Reynolds? Does she actually exist, or is she just another of your publicity gimmicks?"

"I know we spent only five days together, but I never took you to have such a closed mind."

He saw that her eyes glistened as if she might shed tears. *Just another ploy!* he thought coldly. "When someone pulls the wool over your eyes, the way you did mine, then I'll accept your definition of closed mind," he said, his mouth tight and his eyes hard. Even as he felt again the attraction he had felt, he told himself that he would never, ever again be taken in by her.

"Look, here's the bread. I'm not lugging it back to Salt Lake. If you don't want to eat it, feed the pigeons." Amanda turned and marched out the door.

Simon stood watching until she got on the elevator. What was her game? He still doubted her story. But her homemade bread was too good to pass up. He'd keep it.

Well, what else had she expected? Amanda could have kicked herself for even making the attempt to see Simon. It had taken all her nerve to act confident, to not break down. And what good had it done? She'd thought he might have softened his stance by now, and the bread could be a peace offering.

The passage of the last four weeks had been agonizingly slow. Nonnie's leg was healing nicely, Amanda had had a good visit with her parents, and Jenny had had a baby girl. Amanda had dutifully sent a gift, privately wishing she'd never heard of the couple or their Idaho farm. She'd wondered where Simon was, what he was doing, and more importantly with whom. The day after Christmas she'd even gone to Park City, hoping she'd see him. Finally, yesterday she'd just decided to take matters into her own hands. She'd bought an airline ticket and baked the bread.

He'd looked so wonderful today. He hadn't needed a dark tailored suit to give him an air of authority, of being in charge. His refusal to listen to her or accept her bread, however, showed a hard, ruthless streak that hadn't been evident as they'd made candy and cookies.

Pulling her gloves on, she pushed the outside door open and hailed a cab. Since San Francisco wasn't any warmer than Salt Lake, and she had no desire to shop, she might as well return home. She wondered if Simon had read *People,* and found out the story had never been run. She'd killed the article in December as soon as she had returned to Salt Lake.

Four hours later she entered her apartment. Sagging against the door, she wondered why she had gone to San Francisco? She felt like a fool. She'd practically worn her heart on her sleeve, and Simon had rejected her.

She sighed. Images of the time she'd spent at the Canfields' flashed painfully through her mind, and she was filled with regret and longing. She could envision how spring would come to the farm, and the fact that she and Simon wouldn't be a part of it was hard to bear.

She stretched out on the couch to watch reruns of her favorite TV show. When the first commercial came on, she sat up abruptly. Was that "Rob" raving about pizza? She moved closer to the screen. It was! She wondered if this was the commercial that had kept him from leaving for the farm on time. Just in case, she was never buying that particular brand of pizza again.

Two days later, Amanda stood in her office carefully studying the pages of the April issue. Each one had been tacked up on the wall, and she switched them around, striving for balance in the magazine's composition.

Hearing someone enter, she glanced up, then froze. Simon! Amanda felt the blood drain from her face. After his reaction to

176

the bread, what was he doing here? Sparks of anger glinted from the dark depths of his blue eyes, and his lips no longer curved provocatively, but were rigid with dislike.

Nervously, Amanda took a step backward. Simon followed. He stopped short and glanced around. Thank goodness he wasn't in her apartment. She'd gotten rid of the manzanita tree, but she cringed at the thought of his seeing the candy canes and the felt ornaments they'd made hanging on the wall. They would be a dead giveaway of her feelings.

"Why didn't you tell me who you were?" he demanded, advancing still closer.

Amanda took another step backwards. Her knees buckled against a couch, and she stumbled onto it. Feeling very much at a disadvantage with Simon staring down at her, still glowering, she stood up and stared back. He'd taken her by surprise, but she refused to let him put her on the defensive.

"If you remember, you never gave me a chance. You were too busy condemning me." She thrust out her chin defiantly.

"Becki told me that you were Amanda Richards, editor-in-chief of *Today's Home*." He said the last words scornfully. "No wonder you were concerned about publicity."

"That's right. But why didn't you just ask me who I was?"

"Easier said than done. When I discovered we weren't in *People,* I wanted to find out why. Naturally, I called the magazine. I didn't know your name and it took me until yesterday to get through to Becki. She seemed overjoyed to hear from me, and she informed me you were actually Amanda Richards." He gave her a piercing look. "Is anything you told me about you the truth, or was it made up to go along with Laura Reynolds?"

"It's all true, except I didn't come to Utah to write a column. I came to edit *Today's Home.*"

He looked cynical. "I find it hard to believe someone would hire a twenty-four-year-old ex-UCLA songleader to edit a large magazine."

"I was twenty-seven years old, and—" she was loathe to admit the next part "—the publisher was a family friend. Plus *Today's Home* was a small regional publication then."

Simon's eyes gleamed cynically. "Now I understand why you'd do anything for publicity."

"This magazine has been my life for the last five years," Amanda defended herself. "I've felt a great deal of pressure to prove myself with the success of the magazine. I come in earlier and stay later than any other staff member." She spoke quietly.

"Laura Reynolds is my grandmother. Entertaining a house full of company delights her, so I asked her if she wanted to do it. Of course, she'd said yes. Then on her way to buy you and Paul presents, she slipped and broke her leg. Do you think she would let us cancel? No! She'd already invited you and she was not disappointing you. Nonnie insisted I pretend to be her. My granddad insisted. When I talked to you, you sounded so excited, I couldn't cancel the plans."

She looked into his eyes. The dark blue gaze seemed unfathomable, and she was beginning to feel like a fool for revealing herself this way, but she had to convince him of her sincerity. "I really believed we could give you the holiday of your dreams. Confidentially," she pulled a face, "if you hadn't known how to build a fire and cook on a wood range, we would probably have frozen to death the first night!"

Simon's face showed a glimmer of interest. "Do you mean to tell me you couldn't even do all those things you were determined to entertain me with?"

"Well, I could with a lot of help from the Silverspoon and Nonnie's kitchen. It was a production of the entire staff," Amanda explained. At least he was willing to hear her out this time.

Simon's eyes widened, as comprehension dawned. "No wonder your neighbor was afraid of getting tipsy on the mincemeat. It wasn't your grandmother's recipe."

Amanda nodded with a wry grin. "That's right."

"After that ridiculous Fox and Geese game and what happened

between us, why didn't you tell me the truth?" he demanded impatiently.

"When?" Amanda asked impatiently. "I planned to the first moment we were alone. If you remember clearly, the sheriff arrived and it was all over." She waited for Simon's response.

He was silent, until at last he reached toward her. He spoke slowly. "Have you any idea how painful it was to find myself falling in love with a woman I knew I could never have?"

Simon cupped her face between his hands. "Amanda Richards, I love you," he whispered, the fervency of his feelings evident in the huskiness of his voice. He drew her into his arms.

It seemed completely natural to twine her arms around his shoulders. He didn't attempt to kiss her immediately, but his long fingers lingered on the nape of her neck, stroking gently, releasing the pain she'd felt since Christmas. She lifted her mouth for his kiss.

His lips tasted better than she'd ever imagined, sending an involuntary ripple of response through her body. Her lips softened as one kiss melted into another. Amanda clung to Simon, filled with wonder, caught in a spiral of shivery sensation that had no beginning and no end.

The world seemed to spin away, leaving only Simon. He held her as if he never wanted to let her go. Finally, he lifted his head a whisper away. "Do you have any idea how much I've wanted to hold you like this?"

"Do you know how much I've wanted you to?"

Moving a fraction of an inch away, he said, "Can you cook at all?"

Amanda said hesitantly, knowing how much he wanted a traditional wife, "Barely."

"Thank goodness. To be perfectly honest, after five days of cooking and baking, I was getting a little bored."

Amanda pulled back and tapped his arm smartly. "Bored? How dare you say that after all you put me through? Talk about deceit. You acted as if you loved every minute of it!"

"I was just being the perfect guest," he said piously, pulling her closer.

"Let me assure you of one thing—you were never that!" She laughed. "Actually the enthusiastic way you wanted a traditional wife worried me. After one disastrous relationship where I attempted to be somebody I wasn't, I swore never again."

"Don't worry, you're just what I want." The midnight blue of his eyes glittered. "And if worse comes to worse, I'll do the cooking. After all, I've got Laura Reynolds's cookbook!"

"Let me warn you that that's exactly what I thought too. One thing a week at Spindrift Farm taught me: being able to read does not a Laura Reynolds make."

"Minor details."

Simon's arms tightened, and his lips met hers again.

Epilogue

"...From our house to yours—Merry Christmas." Amanda tossed *Today's Home* aside and watched while her husband packed a swim suit and some brightly colored shirts in his suitcase. "Nonnie's letter is as enthusiastic as ever, the only difference is—we're not living it in person. I think I managed to put a damper on some of her more traditional ideas with some judicious editing."

"Just remember if it hadn't been for her column and all the memories it brought back, we'd have never met." Simon grinned at his wife as she lay stretched out on the bed. "Are you sure you never edited any articles on the perfect way to pack a suitcase?"

"No, but I can give you some encouragement." She slid off the bed and wound her arms around his neck. "Thanks for agreeing to spend Christmas in St. Thomas."

"I checked it out and they haven't had a rebellion in sixty years. So we'll probably be safe." He pulled her to him and held her tightly in his arms. "It's the least I could do after you spent last year at Canfields' farm, and the way you gave up your job to be in San Francisco with me." His lips touched her eyes and the tip of her nose before moving to the corners of her mouth in little butterfly kisses.

"Don't you know you're worth it?" Amanda pulled his head closer, and her heart sang as the kiss deepened.

The End

Dear Reader:

I'm sharing some of my favorite Christmas recipes with you. While I'm not as good a cook as Laura, I'm a lot better than Amanda!

Enjoy,

Beverly

Labor of Love Caramels

Note: These caramels are wonderful but very labor intensive. You need time and a strong arm—or someone to spell you off on the stirring.

4 c. sugar
2 c. white corn syrup
1/2 tsp. salt
1 quart whipping cream
1 can evaporated milk
1 tsp. vanilla
1 c. chopped nuts

Mix sugar, syrup, salt, and 2 c. of the cream into a medium saucepan. Slowly bring to a boil over medium heat. After the mixture comes to a good rolling boil, slowly add cream, but do not let the mixture stop boiling. Let it cook until it starts to thicken, stirring constantly. Slowly add evaporated milk. Cook to 232 degrees or a firm ball. Add vanilla and nuts. Pour into a greased pan (9x12) and let stand until firm. Cut into squares and roll in wax paper.

Viennese Sandwich Cookies
Makes 3 dozen

1 c. (2 sticks) unsalted butter, room temperature
1 c. sugar
1 egg yolk
1 t. vanilla
2 c. flour
Sugar
2 c. powdered sugar
1/2 c. (1 stick) unsalted butter, room temperature
2 to 4 T fresh lemon juice
2 squares semi-sweet chocolate
1 T butter
Garnish
Chopped nuts, vari-colored nonpareils or shredded
  coconut

Cream together butter and sugar. Add egg yolk, vanilla and flour, mixing thoroughly. Chill at least 2 hours. Make 72 balls of dough the size of small walnuts. Place 2 inches apart on ungreased cookie sheets. Dip bottom of small glass into sugar and use it to flatten each ball to a thickness of 1/8 inch. Bake 10 to 12 minutes at 325° until cookies are lightly colored with slight brown edges. Do not overbake. Place on cooling rack.

Cream powdered sugar and butter. Add lemon juice to taste (it should be tart). Spread a teaspoonful on half the baked cookies. Cover each one with another cookie, making a sandwich.

In double boiler heat chocolate and butter until just melted. Dip an edge of each cookie sandwich into chocolate, then into nuts, nonpareils or coconut. Place on cooling rack to set.

Store in tightly covered container, layered with sheet of waxed paper, or freeze.

Thumbprints

2/3 c. butter

1/3 c. granulated sugar

2 egg yolks

1 t. vanilla

1/2 t. salt

1 1/2 c. flour, sifted

2 egg whites, beaten

3/4 c. finely chopped walnuts

Cream together butter and sugar, beating until fluffy. Add egg yolks, vanilla and salt, beating well. Gradually add flour, mixing well.

Preheat oven to 350°. Shape dough into small balls, dip in egg white, then roll in chopped walnuts. Place 1 inch apart on greased cookie sheet and press down center with thumb. Bake for 15 to 17 minutes. Cool slightly and remove from pan and cool on cookie rack. Fill thumbprints with butter-cream frosting.

Triple Chocolate Fudge
Makes 2 9x13-inch pans

4 1/2 c. sugar

1 t. salt

1/2 c. (1 stick) butter

1 13 oz. can evaporated milk

1 12 oz. bag of semi-sweet chocolate chips

2 4 oz. bars German Sweet chocolate, broken into
    1-inch chunks

17 oz. milk chocolate, broken into 1-inch chunks or
    milk chocolate chips

1 1/2 7-oz. jars marshmallow cream

2 t. vanilla

4 c. coarsely chopped toasted nuts

In 6-quart Dutch oven, combine sugar, salt, butter and milk. Bring to simmer, stirring constantly, over medium heat. *As soon as the first bubble is seen*, boil the mixture *exactly* 8 minutes. Remove from heat immediately. Quickly stir in remaining ingredients.

Blend thoroughly. Pour into two oiled 9x13-inch pans. Cover with foil and refrigerate until firm. Slice as desired. Bring to room temperature before serving for fullest flavor.

Store in refrigerator or freezer.

Butternut Cookies
Makes about 6 dozen

3/4 c. butter or margarine
1/2 c. confectioners sugar
1 t. vanilla
1 3/4 c. sifted flour
1 c. chopped pecans
1 6 oz. pkg. butterscotch chips
Confectioners sugar (for coating)

Cream butter and 1/2 cup confectioners sugar until light and fluffy; add flavoring.

Stir in flour, pecans and chips; blend well. Form dough into tiny balls; place about 1 inch apart on ungreased baking sheet. Bake in moderate oven (350°) about 10 minutes. *Do not brown.*

Roll cookies in confectioners sugar while warm. Cool on racks.

Pat's Sugar Cookies

Cream together thoroughly:
    1/2 c. shortening
    1/2 c. margarine
    2 eggs

Stir in:
    2 T milk or cream
    2 t. vanilla
    1 t. desired flavoring;
    lemon extract, almond extract, etc.

Sift together and add to creamed mixture:
    3 1/2 c. flour (more can be added to make a stiffer dough)
    1/2 t. baking powder
    1/2 t. salt

Mix thoroughly and then chill about 2 hours. Roll dough thin (1/4"), cut into shapes. Place on greased cookie sheet and bake at 400° (only until edges begin to turn a very light brown). With a flat spatula remove carefully from sheet and cool on a cloth covered board. Frost with powdered sugar glaze.

Glaze

Mix powdered sugar with a small amount of water to the consistency of thick cream. Color with desired food color and dip face of cookies into glaze. Let dry on waxed paper. Store in a covered container.

About the Author

A native Idahoan, Beverly King currently resides in Salt Lake City where she teaches the resource classes at Emerson Elementary School. When asked about her college education, she laughingly admits that she has attended "nearly every university in the West." Ultimately, she graduated from Utah State University and went on to do graduate studies in Special Education at Brigham Young University.

Bev naturally enjoys reading, particularly mysteries and legal thrillers. She also loves reading cookbooks, making cookies, and collecting angels and Christmas ornaments. She says, "I'm a television news junkie and never miss a do-it-yourself program."